All-American Male

Men In Love and Lust, Volume 1

Michael Bracken

Published by Untreed After Dark, 2023.

Also by Michael Bracken and Untreed Reads
Chalkers
"Jimmy's Jukebox," in the anthology *Peace, Love, and Crime: Crime Fiction Inspired by the Songs of the '60s*
"Ray's Dad's Cadillac," in the anthology *The Beat of Black Wings: Crime Fiction Inspired by the Songs of Joni Mitchell*
"The Downeaster 'Alexa,'" in the anthology *Only the Good Die Young: Crime Fiction Inspired by the Songs of Billy Joel*

For Temple
My Love, My Muse, My Everything

Introduction

A good story is a good story, whether it has erotic content or not. And the pieces included in this collection are good stories.

Of course, I may be biased, because several of them were included in anthologies I edited for Cleis Press. But the experience of putting together those volumes, as well as writing my own gay erotica, has given me a good sense of what makes a story sexy, intriguing, and worth reading.

My first published story, under the pseudonym Dirk Strong, was called "The Cop Who Caught Me" and sold to *Mandate*, a gay magazine that combined sexy picture layouts with erotic fiction. That was over thirty years ago, and writing that story, and many others, gave me the entrée I needed to begin editing those Cleis anthologies.

A good story needs to be well-written. Michael Bracken writes strong, propulsive sentences with great descriptions that bring the reader right into the characters' bedrooms—or wherever else they're getting it on.

Here's an example from "Soaring":

"The door of the honeymoon suite had barely closed behind the bellman when I pulled Scott into my arms and kissed him long and hard. Over the course of our developing relationship, we had kissed many times, but never like this, never as a married couple."

It's a wonderful transition from the careful, closeted sex the couple have experienced before their wedding, into their new world as legal spouses.

That's another of the delights of this collection—the way it moves so seamlessly from casual college encounters through Don't Ask, Don't Tell, and the legalization of marriage, all the while taking us on an erotic journey rooted in characters who are very real.

That's important to the reader. We want to feel immersed in stories about real people who have great sex—something we might strive for ourselves, if only we meet the right guy who has the right equipment. Bracken's characters jump off the page, like the college students of "All-American Male," many of whom are experiencing their first time with another man. In "Learning Curve," Carl says, "Dr. Maeyer was older than any man I'd ever been with, but still young enough that I enjoyed his flirtations. His approach was unlike that of guys my age, much more subtle and refined." And Bjorn Maeyer certainly has much to teach him—which we get to witness.

I'm a fan of a well-developed setting, too. While most of these stories are rooted in Texas, Bracken has the ability to bring you almost anywhere in the world, from the inside of a UHF TV station to a house on the Jersey shore. The stories range in time, too, and yet you always know where and when you are.

It's no surprise that Bracken has written and published so many stories in so many venues, and has frequently won awards and been short-listed for others.

One of the things I love about Bracken's stories is the way his language suits the setting. In "Boys of Summer," Carl, the narrator, says, "That didn't slow us down none. We just stripped down to our altogether and let our peckers flap in the wind as we waded into the cool, spring-fed creek."

Then the more sophisticated narrator of "Summer Folk," a recent college graduate with a degree in English, says, "Bag boy wasn't on my grandmother's shopping list so, no matter how appealing I found Tony, he was a seductive treat best left at the grocery store. I said, 'I have to go.'"

The variety of language is one of the delights of the collection and says so much about the characters. In "Creosote Flats and the Big Spread," Stephen Chambers says, "I'd spent the previous day at the salon, where I'd had my hair styled and my eyebrows sugared. I looked fabulous, but fabulous wouldn't last long without air conditioning." That tells us all we need to know about him, especially after his car breaks down and he stumbles upon a cowboy named Carl Rogers, whose friends call him Buck.

And lest you think the writing isn't sexy, consider this passage from that story. "Shampoo ran down Buck's powerful chest, and my gaze followed it over his six-pack abs, through the dark thatch of his pubic hair, and down the length of his thick phallus. I won't say he was hung like a horse, but I'm certain more than a few ponies would be jealous of what I saw dangling between Buck's thighs. I know it took my breath away."

The repartee is equally sprightly, as in this passage from "What Springs Up."

"You look like you could use some help," he said.

The bulge in his shorts seemed to be enlarging, and I wet my lips before answering. "Do you have the right tool?"

He smiled. "There's only one way to find out."

We were obviously thinking the same thing. I removed my gloves and reached for his zipper.

"Not out here," Nicolas said. He took my hand and helped me to my feet. "The tool shed."

If you aren't eager to follow them into that shed, then you should check your own tool to make sure it's working right.

Cowboys, college kids, military men—whatever your interest, you'll find it within these pages. And I hope you'll enjoy them.

—Neil S. Plakcy
Hollywood, Florida

Learning Curve

I first met Dr. Bjorn Maeyer at the annual Christmas party he hosted for his creative writing students the last weekend before finals. Not one of Dr. Maeyer's students, I had been the plus one of my roommate, Bernie, when his girlfriend backed out at the last minute due to a headache and upset stomach likely caused by overindulgence of alcohol at the previous evening's multi-fraternity Christmas party.

Dr. Maeyer lived in a three-story Victorian near campus, in a neighborhood where one couldn't spit without hitting university faculty and their families. Despite biting cold wind and snow flurries, we walked to his home and were greeted at the front door by one of Bernie's classmates, a self-identified poet whose only hope of success would be to write quatrains for greeting cards, who directed us to the cloakroom where we unburdened ourselves of our overcoats and galoshes.

I parted company with Bernie almost immediately upon stepping into the living room when an excessively endowed brunette noticed Bernie was sans girlfriend and dragged him to an unoccupied window seat that overlooked the side yard. I continued through the living room and into the dining room, where an impressive spread of hors d'oeuvres was being picked over by starving young writers of all genres.

I filled a small plastic plate with shrimp and cocktail sauce and continued through to the kitchen where I found an array of soft drinks. I was pouring myself a Dr Pepper when a deep voice behind me said, "I don't believe we've met."

I turned to find myself looking up at Dr. Maeyer. Broad-shouldered and thick-chested, he stood a good three inches taller than me. His blond hair and Vandyke beard had been recently trimmed, and he wore a tweed jacket with leather elbow patches over a festive green turtleneck, in many ways the cliché of an English professor.

"You're not in any of my classes," he said.

"I'm Bernie Schwarz's roommate," I said. I left my Dr Pepper on the counter and stuck out my hand. "Carl McGregor."

When the creative writing professor clasped my hand in both of his I felt an unexpected tingling course throughout my body, something I hadn't felt since breaking up with David the previous summer. I also felt the front of my jeans begin to tighten.

"Plan to take any of my classes?"

"Sorry," I said, "but no. I have one semester left before graduation, and I finished all my English requirements last year."

"Too bad," he said. His blue eyes twinkled with insinuation. "There's so much I could teach you."

A pudgy undergrad with hors d'oeuvre stains on his reindeer tie interrupted us to ask the professor to mediate an argument about the intimacy differences between fiction written in first-person and fiction written in third-person.

"We'll talk later," Dr. Maeyer said before releasing my hand and turning away to play dutiful host to his students.

I retrieved my drink and returned to the living room in time to see Bernie and his brunette classmate engaging in a little tongue wrestling under a sprig of mistletoe. Though I wondered if the brunette's tongue had pushed all thoughts of Bernie's girlfriend from his mind, I didn't ask. I squeezed past them into the library, where I found several comfortable chairs and floor-to-ceiling shelves filled with paperback mysteries.

After finishing my shrimp, I wiped my fingers with a napkin and began examining the books. Because my uncle had been a fan of private eye novels and had given me several over the years, I recognized the names of some of the authors.

"Surprised?"

I turned to see Dr. Maeyer standing behind me. "Not what I expected. Where're Chaucer and Dante and Shakespeare?"

"In the university library where they belong," he said. "Do you like old writers?"

"Some," I said. "If they're not too old."

We were interrupted again, and I was left pondering how I would have responded if we hadn't been. Dr. Maeyer was older than any man I'd ever been with, but still young enough that I enjoyed his flirtations. His approach was unlike that of guys my age, much more subtle and refined. But despite the way he made me feel, there was nothing I could do right then. I returned my attention to the shelves filled with stories of crime and punishment.

The rest of the evening proceeded along the same lines. The professor and I would find ourselves alone for a moment, he would flirt, and then we would be interrupted. After I had wandered through all the rooms on the main floor and eaten my fill of hors d'oeuvres, I returned to the library. I settled into one of the overstuffed chairs with a full glass of Dr Pepper and a Gold Medal paperback almost three times my age. I intended to just thumb through the book, but I soon found myself engrossed in the story.

I didn't realize the Christmas party had wound down until Dr. Maeyer stood in the doorway between the living room and the library and said, "The party's over, my new young friend."

I looked up from the book. "Already?" I asked. "Where's Bernie?"

"He left with Sarah Michelle."

"Then I'd best be leaving, too."

I closed the paperback—disappointed that I'd not been able to finish it—stood and returned it to the shelf. As I stepped past Dr. Maeyer on my way to the living room, he stopped me with a hand to my arm.

He pointed up and I saw the mistletoe. Then he caught the back of my head in one hand and covered my mouth with his. The Vandyke tickled but I didn't resist. In fact, I pressed against him, feeling his erect cock pressing against my thigh. My own cock rapidly inflated.

Every relationship goes through a learning curve, and I had the feeling the learning curve was about to begin. I parted my lips and his tongue quickly found mine in a deep, tongue-twisting kiss that took my breath away. When it finally ended, I pulled away and looked up into his eyes. I could see my own desire reflected back at me, and I knew he wanted me as much as I wanted him.

"Come upstairs," he said.

I followed him to his bedroom on the second floor. Once there, he shook off his tweed jacket and laid it thoughtfully over the back of a chair. He peeled off the green turtleneck, and it joined the jacket. Shoes, socks, pants, and underwear followed. His thick cock jutted up from a nest of blond pubic hair, one of several generational differences I noticed as the evening progressed.

Dr. Maeyer settled onto the chair, wrapped his fist around his cock, and stroked it slowly as I stripped for him. I didn't organize my discarded clothing as neatly as he did. Instead, I dropped everything in a heap on the floor.

Unlike the professor, I carefully groomed my pubic area daily, keeping it hair-free. My cock appeared even larger than it was because it had no competition from the underbrush, but even so I could tell I wasn't quite as well endowed as the professor.

I knelt on the carpet between the professor's legs and pushed his hand aside. With the tip of my tongue, I drew a wet line from his ball sac up the underside of the shaft. Then I took the swollen purple head of his cock into my mouth at the same time I wrapped my fist around the base. As I pumped my fist up and down his length, a bit of pre-come oozed from the tip and I licked it away.

"That the best you can do?" Dr. Maeyer asked as he rested one hand on the back of my head.

I knew what he wanted so I took another half-inch of cock into my mouth before drawing back and letting my teeth catch against the swollen glans. I did it again, taking only that extra half-inch before drawing back.

The professor applied more pressure against the back of my head, encouraging me to accept more of his length into my oral cavity. I pumped my hand faster, trying to make the professor come before he could make me take the entire length.

When I felt him tighten, I knew he was coming. I tried to pull away, but the professor kept a firm grip on the back of my head as he came in my mouth. I'd never let David come in my mouth—I'd never let any of my lovers do that—but the professor hadn't given me a choice.

I swallowed and swallowed again, but I couldn't swallow fast enough and some of the professor's come leaked from my mouth and oozed down the length of his cock shaft to dampen the blond nest of his pubic hair. When his cock finally stopped spasming in my mouth, Dr. Maeyer released his grip on the back of my head. I pulled away and sat on the carpet, looking up at him.

As I wiped my mouth with the back of my hand, he said with a smile, "I do have a lot to teach you."

"Are you planning to grade me?" I toyed with my erect cock, stroking it slowly as we spoke.

He smiled. "I think you know how you're doing."

I returned his smile.

"There's lube in the top drawer," he said, pointing to the nightstand.

I crossed the bedroom to the nightstand and returned with the lube. He had me squeeze some on my fingers and slather it on his thick cock. As I did, his tool slowly regained its previous stature. Then I squeezed another glob onto my fingers, reached behind my ball sac, and coated my ass crack with it.

Dr. Maeyer sat up and reached for me. He spun me around and then gripped my hips and pulled me backward into his lap. His lube-coated cock thrust up between my thighs, prodding at the underside of my sac. I reached between my legs and repositioned myself so that the spongy-soft head of his hard member pressed against my sphincter.

Then, as he held my hips and pulled me down, my ass hole opened to him. Soon the professor's entire cock was buried deep in my ass. He reached around me and took my cock in his fist. As I worked my hips back and forth, he pistoned his hand up and down the length of my shaft.

I couldn't restrain myself and I came quickly, sending a thin stream of jizz shooting across the room but not quite reaching the bed. As soon as I came, he released my cock and grabbed both my hips, pushing me up and pulling me down. I rode his rod like a cowboy on a bucking bronc, the damp nest of his pubic hair tickling my ass each time I slid down his cock.

He began to pump his hips, thrusting his missile upward to meet my descending ass, and then he came. He fired a thick wad of spunk into my ass. As he did that, he pulled me backward until I was resting against his chest, and he had his arms wrapped around me. He kissed my neck and his Vandyke tickled me again.

I lay back against him until his cock finally softened and slipped free. Then we moved to his bed, where Dr. Maeyer held me, kissed me, and fondled me, but we didn't have sex again. Before long we both fell asleep.

* * *

I woke first the next morning. I gathered my clothes, crept downstairs, and dressed in the library. I quickly finished reading the paperback I had started the night before and then retrieved my overcoat and galoshes for the trek across campus to my apartment.

Bernie was already up when I arrived. "Where have you been?" he asked.

"I met someone last night."

"You, too?"

I didn't tell him it was his creative writing professor.

"What'd you think of the party?" he asked. "Dr. Maeyer throws one every Christmas. It's the highlight of the year for some of his students."

I wondered if it was the professor's present to himself, a way to entice fresh meat to his house without seeming creepy. At the same time, he'd been quite careful to ensure that I had never been and would never be one of his students before he put the moves on me, the only way he could ensure not to run afoul of the university's prohibition about instructors having relations with their students.

Without much prompting, Bernie told me a little more about Dr. Maeyer while I made toaster waffles for breakfast. According to my roommate, the professor claimed to be writing his second novel—the first had been published by a small press shortly before the university hired him twenty years earlier—but no one had ever seen even the roughest draft or faintest inklings of an outline.

"But he's a good teacher," Bernie concluded. With Dr. Maeyer's encouragement, he'd had two short stories published in the university's literary magazine and had another rejected by the *New Yorker*. "We've all learned a lot from him."

Dr. Maeyer had certainly taught me a few things during the one night I had known him. I wondered if there was more he could teach me, so I returned to his home that evening. When he answered the door, I said, "I left without saying good-bye and without leaving my number in case you wanted to contact me."

He clasped my arm, pulled me inside and into his arms. We didn't need mistletoe to jump-start our amorous activities that evening, or any subsequent evening.

Campus emptied quickly a few days later, after finals ended and students left for Christmas break. I packed as if I were leaving town to join my parents in Aspen—so Bernie wouldn't be suspicious—and then spent the break holed up in Dr. Maeyer's Victorian. By the time the new semester began and I'd returned to my apartment, the professor and I had fucked at least once in every room in his house. We had also fucked several times in his third-floor office, where he showed me pages from his stalled novel, the story of a young man's coming out in the fifties.

The professor and I kept our relationship on the down-low for the first half of the semester, but spring break provided another opportunity to spend an extended amount of time together. Bjorn—I'd stopped calling him Dr. Maeyer by then—rented a beachfront condo and we drove down to the coast in his Volvo. The one-bedroom twelfth-floor unit had a private balcony facing the Gulf of Mexico. After we unpacked, we stood on the balcony and watched the sun slide down the evening sky.

Before long I turned to Bjorn, unfastened his pants, and let them fall to his ankles. I hooked my thumbs in the waistband of his boxers and pulled them down as I dropped to my knees. He had changed his grooming habits during the months we'd been together and no longer had an unruly nest of blond hair at the juncture of his thighs. Though he didn't manscape the hair into oblivion the way I did, he now kept it neatly trimmed. I appreciated his new grooming habits because by then I had learned to take his entire length into my mouth without gagging and I didn't have to worry about his pubic hair tickling my nose and making me sneeze the way it had the first time I'd swallowed his entire rod.

As his cock rose to attention, I wrapped my fist around the shaft and pulled back his foreskin to reveal the swollen purple head. I took it in my mouth, hooked my teeth behind the spongy soft glans, and painted it with saliva. Then I slowly took his entire length into my oral cavity before I drew back and did it again.

Before I could make him come, the professor pulled his cock from my mouth and pushed my face away from his crotch. "You're missing the sunset."

After he pulled me to my feet, he kicked off his deck shoes and stepped out of his slacks and boxers so that all he wore was a pale-yellow polo shirt. I took the hint and slipped out of my clothes as well.

Apparently, Bjorn'd had the same idea I'd had because he reached into one pocket of his discarded slacks and pulled out the butt-end of a tube of lube. He spun me around so that we both faced the Gulf of Mexico, and I was pressed against the metal railing while he slathered lube into the crack of my ass and into my sphincter. He eased one finger into me, then drew back and pressed the head of his tumescent cock against my well-lubed ass hole. He eased the full length of his cock into me, and then he grabbed the railing on either side of me and began fucking me.

By then my cock was fully erect and straining for attention. I used one hand to brace myself against the railing and keep the professor from crushing me against it with his powerful thrusts. At the same time, I reached down and took my cock in my hand. As the professor drilled me from behind, I matched his rhythm with my fist. The faster he pumped, the faster I jerked.

I'm not certain who came first—the difference couldn't have been more than a fraction of a second—but as Bjorn slammed into my ass one last time and pressed me tight against the railing, I fired a stream of jizz at the sunset. I watched as the wind caught it and flung it back at the building several floors below us, and then the last rays of daylight disappeared as the sun finally slipped behind the horizon.

A few minutes later we gathered our discarded clothing and went inside. We prepared a late-evening snack, and then headed to bed, tired after the long drive.

* * *

I woke midmorning to find Bjorn sitting at the little table on the balcony wearing nothing but a pair of board shorts and a T-shirt emblazoned with the university logo. He'd brought a hardcopy of his novel manuscript with us, and he was making notes in the margin when I joined him.

He'd begun writing again—he called me his inspiration—and had finally finished the first draft of his second novel. Now he was going through it line-by-line. He was making so many changes that the red pencil he used made the pages look like they were bleeding words.

"There's coffee," he said without looking up.

I refilled his cup and poured one for myself. He'd let me bring several of his mystery paperbacks, so I cracked one open to read until he finished work half an hour later. Then we showered and went in search of somewhere to eat lunch. The rest of spring break was much the same. During the day we visited the beach or did some sightseeing or went shopping. We dined at local restaurants. Each evening we returned to the condo for energetic sex. Despite having more than twenty years on me, the professor always woke first, and he spent the quiet hours of the morning working his way through his novel manuscript while I slept.

By the time spring break ended, Bjorn had finished editing his manuscript. Once home, he began inputting the changes into his computer. He let me read bits and pieces of the novel as he worked through the editing process. Sometimes I think he was trying to impress me and other times I think he was seeking my advice because the novel's protagonist was far closer to my age than to his.

Though we continued to keep our relationship on the down-low through the rest of the semester, we both knew it would soon end. I had several job offers pending, none of them within any reasonable distance of the university.

My parents didn't bother attending graduation, having forgotten to schedule time out from their Caribbean vacation, so my post-graduation celebration was limited to some quick handshakes, high-fives, and backslaps with my friends before they ventured off with their families. I found Dr. Maeyer surrounded by his latest batch of just-graduated creative writing students, many of whom would never again write anything more creative than texts, tweets, and Facebook posts. I had hope for Bernie, though, as he had been admitted to an MFA program whose graduates regularly filled the pages of non-paying literary journals and taught English at universities and community colleges throughout the US.

I didn't interrupt the professor's assurances to the recent graduates' parents that their children were oh-so-creative and oh-so-talented and had oh-such-bright futures ahead of them. Instead, I went directly to Bjorn's house and let myself in.

I still wore my cap and gown when the professor arrived more than an hour later, but I had nothing beneath it. My clothes were folded neatly on the chair where he'd sat the first time we'd made love, and I was waiting on the bed.

When I heard him open the back door, I reached under the robe and lubed myself up. He climbed the stairs and a moment later stepped into the bedroom. "I'm sorry I couldn't get away any sooner," Bjorn said. "Being sociable with all those parents is part of my job."

As he stripped off his cap, robe, and the suit beneath it, I assured him that I didn't mind. He soon joined me on the bed and quickly realized I was naked beneath my robe. He must have had an unspoken fantasy because his cock hardened up immediately when he realized I wasn't planning to remove the gown.

He pushed it up to my waist, revealing my own erection. He kneaded my balls and teased the sensitive spot behind my ball sac. When he realized I had already lubed myself, he tried to roll me over so that he could take me from behind just like he had every time before.

I resisted and said, "I want to watch your eyes."

I spread my legs and Bjorn knelt between them. Then I brought my knees up to my chest and he pressed his tumescent cock against the slick pucker of my sphincter. I grabbed the cheeks of his ass and pulled, forcing his cock deep inside me.

His abdomen trapped my cock between us and, as he pumped into me, it rubbed against my cock. Our sex was hard and fast and filled with the raw emotion of two lovers who thought they would never be together again. The mattress bucked beneath us, the headboard slammed against the wall, and I stared into his pale blue eyes the entire time just as he stared into mine. His expressions were alternately filled with love, desire, and sadness, and I suspected my own expressions mirrored his.

I came first, spewing come between us. Several powerful strokes later, Bjorn came. His eyelids fluttered and then he just closed his eyes as he collapsed atop me. For the first time I saw the crinkles at the corners of his eyes, the gray hair threaded through the thinning blond hair atop his head, and realized that he had grown the Vandyke to draw one's eye away from his slightly sagging jowls.

I kept my knees pulled to my chest for as long as I could. When I finally straightened them, my change in position forced my lover's deflating cock out of me. He rolled to the side, gathered me into his arms, and held me.

"You've been good for me, Carl," Bjorn said as he brushed hair away from my eyes. "I wish you didn't have to leave."

I wished the same, but I knew it was time to go. I had reached the other end of the learning curve and there wasn't much more my lover could teach me. If I remained with him, the differences in our ages would become a wedge between us, and neither of us wanted that.

The next morning, I finished packing my car and drove away. I had a job waiting for me in St. Louis.

We never again spoke, but almost two years after we parted company, I received a package in the mail containing Dr. Maeyer's second novel.

He had dedicated it to me.

All-American Male

I know I should have knocked first, but I didn't. In a rush that Friday evening because the essay in my hand was several hours late, I pushed Professor Cargill's office door open with my free hand and found him cock-deep in the ass of a graduate student he had bent over his desk. The professor's slacks were pooled around his ankles and the graduate student's jeans lay in a heap on the floor beside the desk.

"In or out," the professor commanded without breaking rhythm. "And shut the damned door."

I hesitated. I had never seen two men fucking, and the sight caused my cock to tent the front of my jeans. Then I stepped into the professor's office and closed the door behind me.

The graduate student looked at me and smiled but the professor ignored me as he drove harder and faster into the younger man's ass, finally stopping with one last, powerful thrust and a shiver that ran noticeably through his entire body. After a few moments, he stepped backward and pulled his still-throbbing cock out of the graduate student's ass.

The young man splayed across the professor's desk slowly rose, and I could see that he, too, had come because his dark pubic hair was sticky with his own ejaculate.

"What do you want?" Professor Cargill asked as he pulled up his pants and tucked in his shirt. Across the room the graduate student also dressed.

"I—" I held out the three-page essay I held in one hand. "This was due today, but I couldn't get to class. I thought—"

Cargill's narrow face and neatly trimmed beard gave him a faintly satanic look as he glared at me. "You thought you could turn your paper in late and still get credit?"

"My car broke down on the way back to campus from my part-time job," I explained.

The professor screwed the cap on a tube of lube and tossed it into a desk drawer. Then he held out his hand. "Let me see it."

I handed him my paper. He placed it on his desk and reached for a red pen. Without even looking at what I had written, he scrawled a giant F across the front and handed the paper back to me.

"What does it say in the syllabus?" he said. "Late is late, and all late papers fail."

"But—"

He glared at me, and my erection rapidly shriveled. I didn't know what else to do so I let myself out of his office and walked down the otherwise empty hall. The graduate student followed a few steps behind me and caught me at the stairwell.

"Cargill's a real asshole sometimes," he said. "What class are you in?"

"Intro to Art," I told him.

"I do the grading for that one," he said. "Give me your paper and I'll take care of it."

"But—"

"I doubt if Cargill looked at it long enough to even note your name."

I handed him the paper and he glanced at it.

"Don't worry, Simon, I'll be fair," he said, having read my name on the top sheet. "You'll get the grade your paper deserves, which is hopefully better than what he gave you."

"Thanks," I said.

"Emory," the graduate student said as he held out his hand. "Emory Tucker. My office number's in the campus directory. If you ever need anything, come see me."

I took his hand, felt something sticky glue our palms together, and realized what it was as we shook. I didn't know if it was his ejaculate or the professor's, but it didn't matter. On my way downstairs, I wiped it on my jeans.

* * *

Despite the way Professor Cargill had treated me, I couldn't get the memory of watching him fuck Emory out of my mind, and I tossed and turned through the night, my erection serving as a flesh kickstand that prevented me from rolling over without thrashing. Sometimes I dreamed I was the uninvolved observer just as I had been—but instead of standing idly by, I unzipped my jeans and drew my cock free, wrapped my fist around the stiff shaft, and pumped wildly until I showered the two men with my come. Other times I dreamed I was in Cargill's place behind Emory, slamming my cock into the graduate student's firm ass so hard the desk bucked across the office, and I had to keep stepping forward until, with one last powerful thrust that tore a roar from my throat, I erupted within Emory's ass. Still other times I was in Emory's place, spread-eagle on top of the professor's desk, my trapped cock sliding back and forth on the polished wood as Cargill pounded into me from behind. In this scenario, I demanded that he fuck me harder and faster and deeper until I came all over the desk and Cargill slammed into me one last time before filling my ass with hot come.

I woke the following morning to find my BVDs filled with dried come from my first-ever nocturnal emissions and my thoughts clouded with the realization that my long-unspoken desires had a real place in the new world I'd entered when I'd left my small town for the big city.

The same thing happened again the next night, but not the night after that. Before I went to bed on Sunday, I whacked off in the shower until my arm was too tired to lift and my cock nothing but a raw nub. And I slept without rousing. By the time I slid into my seat in the last row of the lecture hall for Intro to Art that Monday afternoon I had convinced myself that I had my carnal desires under control.

I was wrong. When Cargill swaggered in and mounted the stage, my cock sprang to attention—and it remained that way through most of the hour while Cargill droned on about the random items pictured in an endless stream of slides. I didn't watch the slides as much as I watched the professor, imagining him using his cock to point to the projected images rather than using the laser pointer gripped in his fist.

At the end of class, Cargill had one of the students return our papers while he gathered his notes and departed, and I was pleased to learn that I had received an eighty-nine for my effort. Emory had been true to his word.

The next few days, when I wasn't working at the sandwich shop or hosing down the shower walls with my ejaculate, I holed up in the library, researching a paper for English Lit. I kept thinking about Emory, though, and about his suggestion that I visit him. So, after my last class Thursday, I crossed campus to the Fine Arts Building and descended to the basement where many of the Art Department's graduate students maintained studio offices. Having learned my lesson, I knocked on Emory's door and waited for a response before I pushed it open.

"Simon!" he said as he rose from behind his desk. "I wondered how long it would be before you came to see me."

I didn't respond immediately because I was overwhelmed by the decor. The walls of Emory's office were covered with sketches of nude male torsos representing multiple ethnicities and posed in various positions. But my gaze was more drawn to the diversity of sketched cocks on display. They rose majestically from wild nests of pubic hair or hung flaccid against denuded ball sacs. Circumcised and uncut, flaccid and erect, thick and thin, long and short, they shared space with loose-hanging ball sacs and scrotums tightened by fear or by cold.

I wet my lips and swallowed hard before I turned my attention to Emory. Only a few years older than me, he had a mess of dark hair that he brushed away from his sparkling eyes as we spoke. "I just came by to thank you," I said.

"No thanks necessary." He removed a pile of paper from the only other chair in his office. "Sit."

I looked again at the sketches surrounding me before settling on the edge of the chair. I'd never had such a physical reaction to artwork, and I rested my backpack in my lap to hide my developing erection.

"They're for my masters thesis exhibition," Emory explained in answer to my unasked question. "I use some of the same nude models as the figure drawing classes, and some of these are friends of mine."

"Friends?"

"That's my ex-boyfriend, Theo," he said as he pointed to a thick erection that must have been more than eight inches long. Then he pointed to a flaccid penis that was clearly a grower, not a shower. "And that one should be familiar to you. That's Professor Cargill."

I glanced at him and looked around.

"Sorry," he said with a smile. "No self-portraits."

He had read my mind and I smiled awkwardly.

"You should pose for me sometime."

"Me?" I asked, surprised. "Why me?"

"Because you're imagining yourself up on the wall, wondering how you measure up."

I had been thinking exactly that, but I didn't admit it. Embarrassed that Emory had so easily read my thoughts, I stood to go, keeping my backpack in front of me as I did. "Thanks again for grading my late paper," I said.

"Not a problem," he said with a smile. "Just don't be late again. I might not be able to rescue you a second time."

I let myself out and exited the Fine Arts Building as quickly as I could. College wasn't turning out to be anything like I had expected. My best friend and I had fooled around one evening after we'd stolen a bottle of Jack Daniel's from his father's liquor cabinet, but nothing had ever come of those experiences. Trevor was still set to marry his high school sweetheart that June, and I was just confused.

The dreams continued for the next few nights, only Professor Cargill was no longer in them. Instead, I dreamed of Emory taking me in his studio office, bending me over his desk the way Professor Cargill had taken him, and slamming his cock into my ass while dozens of erect cocks just out of my reach teased me with their presence, all waiting their turn to have me even though they were only two-dimensional sketches.

I finally called Emory and told him I was ready to pose.

* * *

Unlike disrobing in physical education class with a bunch of adolescent boys equally embarrassed at the sight of each other and by our nakedness, this was me removing my clothes in front of a man—only a few years older than me, but a man nonetheless—that I had recently seen bent over my Intro to Art professor's desk taking a cock in the ass and about whom I had been dreaming ever since. Naked, I settled onto a stool in the center of the studio office.

"Are you cold?" Emory asked.

"No," I said. "Why?"

"You seem a little withdrawn."

I glanced down.

"I'm just nervous," I admitted. "I've never done anything like this before."

"Just relax." Emory adjusted a pair of softbox lights. Then he grabbed a sketchpad and a charcoal pencil and settled onto his chair.

As he sketched, I watched his eyes and his hand. I saw the way he glanced at me, and I watched the pencil in his hand dart across the page. As the sketch filled in, his glances grew longer and longer. His attention excited me, and my cock lengthened and stiffened until it jutted upward from my crotch. Flustered, I tried to cover myself with my hand.

"Relax," Emory suggested. "It's okay."

He set aside his sketchpad and crossed the room to me. He placed one hand on my shoulder, his other hand on my opposite arm. The moment had finally come. I thought I knew what he was about to do, and I beat him to it. I stretched up and kissed him.

Emory drew back and stared into my eyes. "Do you think that's why I asked to sketch you?"

Confused and embarrassed, I asked, "Isn't it?"

"You're a cute kid," he said.

I was no kid. I had just turned nineteen.

"But you're not my type. I like older men," Emory said. "They can do more for my career."

"So, you asked me here—?"

"Just to sketch you," he said. "Nothing more."

My cock deflated rapidly. My fantasy of being taken in Emory's studio remained just that, and the sketched cocks staring down at me from the walls seemed disappointed. "You don't want me?"

"Not like that," he said. He grabbed his sketchpad and flipped it around so that I could see what he had drawn. "Like this."

Though I had seen my reflection in the mirror many times, I had never imagined myself the way Emory envisioned me, and I stared at the unfinished sketch until he flipped the page over, repositioned me, and began anew.

Though I posed for Emory several more times before spring break bifurcated the semester, he didn't invite me back after we returned to school. I threw myself into my studies and tried to forget everything that had happened.

* * *

Most of the university's MFA students held their thesis exhibitions in the three-story atrium of the Fine Arts Building, but a select few hold theirs off campus, and that year Emory was among them. Professor Cargill arranged for a downtown gallery to host his *All-American Male*, several dozen sketches selected from among the many I had seen adorning Emory's studio office.

An invitation-only reception kicked off the first evening of the week-long exhibition, and I almost didn't make it, arriving on foot almost thirty minutes after it began because my car sputtered to a halt, and I had to walk the last six blocks to the gallery.

Emory's three faculty advisors were present, as were Professor Cargill and several men and women I did not recognize. I collected a glass of sparkling grape juice from the bar, and I sipped at it as I circumnavigated the room and examined Emory's work.

I had seen many of the sketches before—either when I first visited Emory's office or during some of my subsequent visits when I posed for him—but I had not expected to find myself standing in a public place staring at a larger-than-life-size sketch of my own semi-erect cock. My cheeks warmed and I suspect I was blushing even though I knew no one could identify me from the headless torso on display.

"Like it?" I turned at the sound of Emory's voice. "I think it's one of my best."

In a voice barely above a whisper, I said, "You didn't tell me—"

"What did you think I would do with the sketches when I finished?" he asked. "You knew I was working on my thesis exhibition when you agreed to pose."

"I guess I didn't think," I admitted. I had been too wrapped up in the thrill of exposing myself to another man to think about the consequences of posing, and I wondered how many of the other men attending the reception also had their cocks on display.

Before I could ask, a man Emory's age joined us. He pulled Emory into a familial hug, kissed him on the lips, and said, "Sorry I'm late."

"Stop," Emory said, pushing him away. "You'll upset Cargill."

"You still banging that old queen?"

"Be nice," Emory said as he pressed one finger against the other man's lips. "If it wasn't for Cargill, my work would be lost in the crowd at the atrium."

Then Emory turned to me. "Simon," he said, "this is Theo, my ex."

I couldn't help myself. I glanced at Theo's crotch.

Emory noticed and laughed. "Theo," he said, addressing his ex. "This is the undergrad I wanted you to meet."

Theo looked me up and down. "Well," he said, "isn't this my lucky day."

"I need to mingle," Emory said, excusing himself. "I'll leave you two to get acquainted."

As Emory walked away, Theo said, "We were undergrads together. He went on to grad school and I sold out. I design advertising for a boutique agency nearby." I told him I was one of Professor Cargill's students.

"Emory told me about you walking in on them," he said. "Must have been quite a shock."

I admitted that it had been.

"And a little exciting, too?"

"I couldn't sleep for days." I glanced at Theo. Handsome, almost twenty years younger than Professor Cargill, and, if Emory's sketch was to be believed, much better endowed than the professor. "But why would Emory leave you for someone like that?"

"Cargill's frustrated because he's stuck teaching intro courses," Theo explained. "So, every year he takes some promising young artist under his wing, uses him for a bit, and then discards him. Emory's flipped the script. He's been using Cargill." He made a vague motion with his hand that seemed to encompass everything around us. "It seems to have worked."

We'd been standing in front of Emory's sketch of my naked torso long enough, so Theo put his hand on the small of my back and guided me to the next sketch. This was of a young black man whose cock, though of average proportions, thrust upward from the tight nest of curls at his crotch.

"What about you?" Theo asked, his hand moving lower as he spoke. "What are you looking for?"

Before I could respond, Professor Cargill recognized Theo and interrupted us. As they spoke, he glanced at me. His eyes narrowed as if he was trying to place me but couldn't. Then he dismissed me as unworthy of further thought, finished his brief conversation with Theo, and moved on.

I remained at Theo's side for the rest of the evening, basking in the presence of his effervescent personality, and secretly reveling in his touch.

At the end of the evening, when it was evident that the reception was winding down and I feared I might not be able to get back to campus if I remained much longer, I told Theo I had to leave.

"I'll walk you to your car."

"You might not want to," I said. "My car is six blocks away." I explained why—and that I planned to catch the bus back to campus.

"There's no need for that," he said. "I'll give you a ride."

About half the reception's attendees had already departed, so it was quick and easy to excuse ourselves and make our escape.

In Theo's SUV as we drove away from the gallery, he said, "Are you sure you want to go all the way back to campus? I have an apartment about a mile from here. You could spend the night and we could take care of your car in the morning."

I swallowed hard. "Sure," I said. "We could do that."

* * *

Once inside his dark bedroom with the apartment door locked and the curtains pulled closed, Theo crooked one finger under my chin and lifted it. He stared into my eyes as he wet his lips with the tip of his tongue, and then he leaned forward and kissed me. Trevor and I had kissed when we were drunk on his father's Jack Daniel's, but it was nothing like Theo's kiss. Theo's lips pressed against mine, smashing my lips back against my teeth. He sucked my lower lip into his mouth and gently bit it, and I didn't resist when he thrust his tongue into my mouth.

I had dreamed of a moment like this after seeing Professor Cargill with Emory, and I had dreamed of Emory in his office, and I had dreamed of Emory's sketches coming to life and taking me. At least one of those dreams was coming true as liquid heat surged through my body and my cock responded.

Theo slid one hand between us and cupped my erection through the thin material of my chinos. His grip was firm and confident—so unlike my drunken fumblings with Trevor—and I knew I was in the hands of someone who knew what he wanted. That he was an older man—older than me by a handful of years, at least—and that my first sight of two men fucking was that of a professor and a graduate student with a significant span of years separating their ages, did not escape me.

After unthreading my tie, Theo unbuttoned my shirt and pushed it off my shoulders. I let it slip down my arms and fall to the floor at my feet. He grabbed the hem of my undershirt and lifted it over my head and off my arms. He threw it aside. Then he thumbed my nipples until they stiffened.

I hopped on one foot and then on the other as I pulled off my shoes and tossed them aside. I unbuckled my belt, unbuttoned my pants, unzipped my fly, and dropped my chinos to my ankles. Then I peeled off my socks and my BVDs.

As I undressed, so did Theo. Thanks to posing for Emory, getting naked in front of another man didn't faze me, and I didn't start to get nervous until Theo stripped off his boxer briefs and I realized that Emory's sketch of his ex-lover's cock actually *downplayed* its length and girth.

"You're shaking," he whispered. "Are you nervous?"

"A little," I admitted.

Theo took me into his arms, trapping our erect cocks between us as he drove his tongue into my mouth again, and I couldn't restrain myself. I came.

Embarrassed, I pulled away. "I—I'm sorry—I—"

"It's okay," Theo said as he pulled me back into his arms and brushed his fingers through my hair. "This is your first time, isn't it?"

I nodded—but even as nervous as I was, I couldn't ignore the erection pressed against my abdomen. I dropped to my knees and for a moment just stared at Theo's denuded pubic region, heavy ball sac, and thick cock. I had dreamed about what I would do in this situation, but now that I was here, I had no idea. Theo understood that as he gently guided me. He wrapped his fist around the base of his cock and rubbed the swollen purple head across my lips. I could taste the salty stickiness of his pre-come when I wiped my lips with the tip of my tongue.

He took my hand and wrapped it around the base of his cock, replacing his fist. His cock felt nothing like my cock, even less like Trevor's. I took the fat head between my lips and poked at it with the tip of my tongue. Then I opened my mouth and took the entire thing into my oral cavity. I hooked my teeth behind the glans and licked all the way around his cock head as if it were a flesh lollipop. As I did that, Theo wrapped his hand around my hand and began pumping it up and down the thick shaft of his cock. After a few strokes, I knew what he wanted, and I continued the rhythm on my own.

Theo wrapped his hands around the back of my head and held me as he pushed his cock forward. I took another inch—maybe two—into my mouth until it triggered my gag reflex. Theo quickly drew back.

"I've wanted you ever since Emory first showed me his sketches of you and told me about the look on your face when you found him bent over Cargill's desk," Theo said as he ran his fingers through my hair, and I pumped my fist up and down the length of his thick shaft.

Theo's hips began moving forward and back, his hairless ball sac tightened, and then he came, filling my mouth with his thick, salty come. I couldn't swallow it all and some dripped down my chin.

I held his cock in my mouth until it stopped spasming. Then Theo pulled me to my feet and had me lie facedown on the bed and spread my legs. After he retrieved a tube of lube from the nightstand, he slathered lube between my ass cheeks and over the tight pucker of my ass. He continued massaging my ass hole with lube until I finally relaxed, and he slipped one slickened finger into me.

I gasped and my eyes opened wide in surprise as he pistoned his finger in and out of me at least a dozen times. My cock grew hard and so did his because he withdrew his finger, grabbed my hips and pulled me onto my knees. He stepped between my legs and pressed the fat head of his cock against my lube-slickened sphincter. Then he pushed into me slowly until his entire length was buried in my ass hole. He drew back and did it again. He slowly increased the speed of his movements until he was fucking me so hard my ass cheeks were slapping him with each thrust. I reached down and grabbed my erect cock, wrapped my fist around it, and matched Theo's increasing speed.

I came first, firing a thick wad of come onto the bed sheet, and then Theo came, sending his warm come deep inside me. He held himself tight against my ass until his cock stopped spasming, and then he pulled it from me.

I rolled over on the bed, satiated in a way I had never been, my dreams having finally become reality. And though a dozen sketches come-to-life weren't lined up waiting to fuck me, I was fully satisfied with the one that had as Theo lay on the bed beside me, took me in his arms, and we fell asleep together.

* * *

Not until the next morning, when sunlight brightened the bedroom through the curtains, did I see hanging from the wall opposite the bed one of Emory's early sketches of me and beneath it a dresser with several framed photos of Emory with Theo, Emory with Cargill, and Theo with Cargill arranged upon it. I discovered that Theo had been one of the art students Cargill had used and discarded, and I realized I had learned a life lesson in relationships far beyond anything I would have expected from my first year in college.

Theo helped me with my car that morning, and we saw each other twice more before the semester ended, but the relationship did not survive my summer at home, and I never saw him again. Emory successfully defended the written portion of his thesis—an exploration of the idea that the male nude is undervalued and underrepresented in modern art in favor of the female nude—and left town with his MFA to teach at a junior college in the Midwest. The *B* I earned from Professor Cargill was in line with my other grades that semester, and it satisfied my parents. Though I saw Cargill on campus occasionally, I never again entered the Fine Arts Building.

I'm a graduate student myself now—working in the English department's writing lab—and I have become the experienced older man I had once lusted after. Why, earlier today I met a freshman who just might need my guidance in the ways of the world.

Maybe I'll show him my collection of Emory's sketches.

Discovering the Underground

The world's largest Baptist university is located on the banks of the Brazos River in the heart of Texas, and official policy does not tolerate sexual misconduct—misconduct that, if discovered, results in sanctions that range from censure to expulsion. I knew this before I applied for admission.

On the theory that first-year students living on campus perform better academically, on-campus housing is mandatory for incoming freshmen. I knew this before I accepted the university's financial aid package.

The university has a thriving underground population of guys like me, guys who have no interest in the coed population. I discovered this shortly after I moved into my dorm room.

My roommate was sitting on his bed, staring at something on his iPhone, when I walked into our room after my first day of class. As I dumped my knapsack on my bed, I asked, "What're you staring at?"

He flipped the phone around so that I could see the photo on the screen. "My best friend," Trevor said. "This is the longest Kevin and I have been apart since we met."

Trevor's best friend was a football player or a wrestler or a weightlifter. Shirtless, he leaned back against the tailgate of a Chevy Stepside. He had muscular arms, broad shoulders and a thick chest that tapered down to a narrow waist, a six-pack with a thin line of hair that trailed down from his navel and disappeared under the waistband of his jeans, and a bulge at his crotch that sent a little shiver up my spine.

"I wouldn't mind having a friend like that," I said, and saw my roommate's eyes narrow as he considered my comment.

He turned the phone back around, changed the screen to a Words with Friends game in progress, and pretended to be studying the screen for his potential next play. We didn't talk about what Trevor's friendship with Kevin meant or about the deeper meaning of my reaction to Kevin's photo until several weeks into the semester. By then Trevor and I had grown more comfortable and realized that we weren't attracted to one another, and felt certain neither of us would open the other's metaphorical closet door for the university's inspection.

"I miss Kevin," Trevor said.

They talked several times each day, so I wondered how it was possible. Then Trevor showed me a sext Kevin had sent earlier that afternoon, a close-up of an erect cock that must have stood seven inches tall, though it may have appeared longer than it really was because Kevin's pubic hair was little more than a five o'clock shadow.

My own cock twitched at the sight. Unlike Trevor, I had left no one at home, and I had been reluctant to approach anyone, even in town, for fear that word would get back to someone at the university. I had been using my memory of the photo I'd seen of shirtless Kevin leaning against his truck's tailgate to fuel my masturbatory fantasies, but this was even better and would fuel my fantasies for the following several weeks. I said, "Won't you see him at Thanksgiving?"

Trevor shook his head. "That's almost two months from now," he said dejectedly. "Besides, my family's all going to my grandmother's house in Florida."

"What about a weekend trip to see him?"

"I can't," my roommate said. "My parents would know if I went home."

"So, invite Kevin here."

"Here? He can't stay here!"

"Not in the dorm," I clarified. "There must be someplace, though."

A few days later I had the answer and shared what I had learned with Trevor. One Saturday evening two weeks after that, Kevin drove from West Texas and rented a room at a little no-tell motel off one of the back roads leading into town, a place where the owner didn't bother checking IDs when guests paid cash.

I'd made certain that Trevor's car wouldn't start that evening, and he called from the parking garage to ask me to take him to the motel where his boyfriend was waiting. I was more than happy to do it and soon I parked in front of Room Six, next to Kevin's Chevy Stepside.

Trevor's boyfriend opened the motel room door when he heard my car doors slam, and he leaned against the doorframe wearing nothing but tight-fitting jeans. He was just as drool-worthy life size as he was on the screen of Trevor's iPhone. With a nod in my direction, he asked, "Who's this?"

"My roommate."

Trevor hurried to Kevin, wrapped his arms around the bigger man, and tried to smother him with kisses. Kevin stepped backward, out of the open doorway, and pulled Trevor inside with him.

Without waiting for an invitation, I followed them into the motel room and found that the two lovers had already fallen across the king-size bed. Trevor was shedding clothes faster than a man afire, and when he was naked, he began pulling at Kevin's jeans.

I had seen my roommate naked on several previous occasions, but I'd only seen photos of Kevin on the tiny screen of Trevor's iPhone. When his erect cock finally sprang free of his jeans, I thought I would swoon. As long and as thick and as hard as I'd expected it to be, his cock had no pubic hair surrounding it to distract from its tumescent glory.

Kevin lay on his back, his cock jutting upward, and my roommate was on all fours beside him, about to take Kevin's cock into his mouth, when I must have done something that reminded him of my presence. Trevor looked over his shoulder at me. "A little privacy, eh?"

With a sigh, I stepped backward and closed the door. Then I sat on the step outside Room Six, leaned against the door, and listened while they consummated their relationship. The familiar sounds emanating from the room made my cock hard, but there was nothing I could do about it right then. So, I watched other motel guests arrive, either separately or together.

A middle-aged man already inside opened the door to Room Seven and greeted a much younger woman who'd hidden her face from me when she tapped on his door, two boisterous cowboys carrying twelve-packs of Lone Star Beer entered Room Two, and I thought I saw the graduate student who taught my Intro to World Religions class slip into Room Twelve. Before I could confirm my suspicions, the door opened behind me, and I had to catch myself to keep from landing on my back.

I turned and looked up at Trevor, who wore nothing but his pants and a satiated grin. He said, "You can come in."

The bed was a mess and Trevor was alone. I could hear the shower through the open door of the bathroom. When Trevor sat on the side of the bed, I sat in the room's only chair, thankfully positioned in such a way that I could look over Trevor's shoulder into the mirror above the dresser and see a reflection of everything happening in the bathroom.

As I watched, Kevin stepped out of the shower and grabbed a towel. Beads of water glistened against his smooth skin and his now-flaccid cock slapped at his thighs as he vigorously dried his hair. He saw me watching his reflection but did nothing to hide his nakedness until he finished drying himself. Then he wrapped the towel around his waist and joined us in the bedroom.

We talked for a bit. Trevor told Kevin all about the university and I learned that Kevin had gone from high school graduation to full-time employment. Before long, the conversation lost steam and Kevin suggested watching a movie.

We sat on the king-size bed, Kevin in the middle, and watched television until Trevor fell asleep. Then Kevin's hand drifted onto my thigh.

My cock, which had been at half-mast ever since settling on the bed next to Kevin, quickly grew to its full length. I was the only one of us fully dressed—Trevor had stripped down to his jockey shorts and Kevin had never put on anything after his shower but the towel around his waist—and I had to shift position to get comfortable. When I did, Kevin's hand moved to my crotch, and he cupped my ball sac through the thick material of my jeans.

Even though what was happening was exactly what I'd been angling for when I'd suggested Trevor invite Kevin to visit and when I had just that afternoon disabled Trevor's car by tinkering with the distributor cap, I tried to pretend it wasn't. Kevin lightly stroked the bulge in my jeans before sliding the zipper open.

I turned to look at him and saw the towel tented over his crotch. He pushed the towel aside with his free hand and revealed the subject of my most recent masturbatory fantasies, so close I could reach out and touch it.

Trevor snored lightly on the other side of Kevin. I nodded toward my sleeping roommate and said, "What about—?"

"I won't say anything if you won't."

I toed off my tassel loafers, unsnapped my jeans, and then lifted my hips so I could slither out of my jeans and boxers without leaving the bed. I kicked them to the floor with my loafers.

As soon as I was settled again, Kevin wrapped his fist around my stiff cock and slid it up and down. My cock wasn't nearly as long as his, so his fist didn't have far to travel.

I reached for his tumescent erection, but he pushed my hand away. I wasn't sure why he did that, but by then I was more interested in what he was doing to me. He had a firm grip and the faster he stroked, the tighter he gripped my cock.

Then, just as I came, he released his grip and I sprayed come all over my T-shirt. Before my cock stopped spasming, Kevin said, "There's lube in the bathroom." We slipped out of bed and quietly crossed the room. I pushed the bathroom door closed and snapped on the light while Kevin grabbed a tube of lube from the sink top.

He spun me around and slathered lube into my ass crack, massaging it into my sphincter until he could easily slip one finger into me. Then I braced myself against the sink and he took me from behind, sinking his long, thick cock deep into my well-lubed shit chute.

He drew back until just his fat cock head remained inside me, and then he drove forward again, keeping a slow, steady rhythm. I watched the reflection of his face in the mirror. When he caught me, he smiled.

I don't know if it was because I hadn't gotten laid in several months, or if I was just turned on by the thrill of fucking my roommate's boyfriend without his knowledge, but my cock head was still twitching from my orgasm in the bed when it started to rise again. I wrapped my fist around it and jerked off while Kevin pounded into me from behind.

I'd never met a guy who could last so long, and I came into my fist before Kevin even began speeding up. His strokes grew harder and faster, slamming into me and slamming me against the sink so hard I expected to see bruises on my thighs when we finished.

With one last powerful thrust, he drove as deep as possible and erupted within me, firing wad after wad of hot come. As his cock spasmed, we stared at the reflections of each other's eyes, and I knew for him, as it was for me, that we'd had a good fuck and nothing more. I didn't have the kind of feelings for Kevin that Trevor did.

After I minute or so, Kevin pulled away, we cleaned up, and we returned to bed. Trevor hadn't even stirred.

Early the next morning, Trevor shook me awake.

"Kevin has to leave soon," he said. "It's a long drive home."

"So?"

"A little privacy?" he said. "We need to say goodbye."

As I sat outside the motel room listening to Kevin and Trevor going at it, I saw one of the religion professors in the doorway of Room Twelve kissing the graduate student I'd seen the previous evening. Trevor was wrapped up in his own little world when we left a little while later, texting Kevin before we were even out of the motel parking lot, so I didn't say anything to him about what I'd seen.

Instead, I waited until Monday afternoon during the graduate student's office hours and paid him a visit.

"I saw you Sunday morning," I said after his office door was securely closed behind me, "and you weren't leaving church."

His eyes narrowed and he asked cautiously, "What do you want?"

"I just want to know how you get away with it."

He relaxed, and that's when I learned about the university's thriving underground population of guys like me. With that knowledge, I never lacked for appropriate companionship during the rest of my university stay, and I never again approached my roommate's boyfriend.

Come to Jesus

Tony told everyone I tutored him, even though we both knew he earned his grades without my help, so no one ever questioned why we spent so much time alone in his dorm room. It just seemed easier that way. After all, as a running back for our Baptist university's football team, he needed to maintain his stereotypically macho image, an image Tony cultivated by attending all the right fraternity parties and allowing himself to be seen with some of the campus's most attractive female eye candy hanging off his arm. What no one ever saw was me playing naked center to his quarterback while he called all the plays.

We met by accident when we both pulled an all-nighter at the library studying for finals, and we'd both recognized a mutual attraction that neither of us acted on right away. Tony had been getting all his action away from campus and had no desire to be outed—on purpose or by accident—by hooking up with another college boy. I respected that, but it didn't make me desire him any less. Tony's black coffee to my latte. He's broad-shouldered, with a six-pack abdomen, tight ass, and powerful legs. He keeps his head shaved and has barely visible tattoos on each of his arms that he tells girls are gang tats from the hood. I know they're nothing more than tribal designs he picked out of a tattoo book because he thought they looked cool. He had no more come from the hood than I had and would probably be scared shitless if he ever ran into real gangbangers. He'd grown up in a suburb where his mother taught high school English and his father was a mid-level manager at a bottling plant, and if his mother ever heard the dope way he talked around the white girls who didn't know hip-hop from flip-flop, she would probably wash his mouth out with soap.

I look every bit the studious young man that I am, slender with thick glasses that constantly slide down my nose, with a fashion sense that screams Abercrombie and Fitch instead of Fubu. I can't help it. That's the way I was raised. My father's a thoracic surgeon, my mother is his office manager, and my sister and I were always on display at this social event or that.

Tony and I crossed paths several more times after that night in the library because I made it a point to be where I knew he would be. I even started attending the same Baptist church as Tony, the one most of the school's jocks attended in order to maintain the facade that they were true believers, not just athletically gifted young men and women looking for a free ride through the religious university that had recruited them and then put them on display every week during their respective sports' seasons.

I never made a play for Tony, but I let him know in subtle ways that I was interested, and I let familiarity breed curiosity. He finally cornered me after Sunday school. We had remained behind after class, having volunteered to straighten up the room while our classmates hurried to the sanctuary to listen to the ravings of a right-wing pastor crisscrossing the country inciting opposition to same-sex marriage.

While I stacked Bibles in the corner, Tony locked the classroom door. When I heard the lock snap into place, I turned.

"You've been stalking me," he said. "Why?"

"You know why," I said as I closed the distance between us. "You want me as much as I want you."

"You think I'm that way?"

"I know you are, Tony. You can't hide it from me any longer." I reached down between us and cupped his package. He wore boxer briefs beneath his slacks, and they bunched everything together nicely. I stroked the bulge of his cock with my thumb, and it quickly reacted.

He didn't resist so I opened his pants and let them slide to his ankles. After I hooked my thumbs in the waistband of his boxer briefs, I pulled them down and dropped to my knees in front of him.

His thick, uncircumcised cock stood at attention in front of my face, and I admired it for a moment. Then I wrapped one fist around his stiff shaft and pulled the foreskin away from his swollen cock head. I bent forward, took his cock head in my mouth, and hooked my teeth behind the spongy soft cap. I had intended to lick away the glistening drop of pre-come, but Tony had other ideas. He wrapped his powerful hands around the back of my head and shoved his cock deep into my oral cavity. Then he drew back and did it again, knocking my glasses askew.

His heavy nut sac slapped against my chin every time he thrust forward, his untamed pubic hair tickling me with each thrust. I slid one hand between his thighs and tickled the sensitive spot behind his nut sac, sliding the tip of my middle finger closer and closer to his sphincter as he began fucking harder and faster.

When I shoved my finger into him, sinking it to the second knuckle, he slammed his cock into my mouth, moaned with pleasure, and came hard. He fired wad after wad of hot spunk against the back of my throat and I did my best to swallow it all without gagging.

A minute passed, maybe two, and then he released his grip on my head. I drew back but did not release my oral grip on his rapidly deflating cock until I had licked it clean. Then I stood, licked my lips, straightened my glasses, and stared deep into his eyes.

I said, "Don't tell me you haven't been dreaming about that since the first time we met."

Tony pulled up his pants and refastened them. "Let's get out of here."

He unlocked the door and we headed for the exit. The football team's placekicker stepped out of the restroom as we passed. "You're going the wrong way," he said. "You're missing a great sermon."

"I don't think we're missing anything," Tony told him.

The church was located just off-campus, so we had walked to the service that morning. We hurried across campus and Tony led me to his dorm room, a room he wasn't obligated to share because he was on the football team.

After he had the door closed and locked behind us, he pulled me into his arms and kissed me hard and deep. We quickly stripped off each other's clothes, our fingers and tongues exploring one another's bodies as we went. We paused only long enough for Tony to dig in his top dresser drawer for a tube of lube.

He squirted a glob on the end of his finger and then he spun me around and bent me over the end of his bed. He didn't waste any time slathering lube over my sphincter. As he slid one finger into me, my cock began to stiffen. By the time he was able to slide a second finger into me, my cock was hard enough to play on the defensive line.

His cock had grown hard again, and he pressed his cock head against my ass hole. I pushed back against him as he pressed forward and soon his uncut cock was buried inside me. My entire body quivered with delight as he grabbed my hips and began fucking my ass like no guy had ever fucked it before. He was hard and fast and rough, and as he pounded into me, I grabbed my own cock and fist-fucked myself.

I came first, spewing spunk all over his unmade bed, and then he came, slamming into me one last time before filling my ass with his hot spunk.

I would have collapsed on his bed, but Tony still had a hold of me, his thick fingers gripping my hips as tightly as he was known to grip any football placed in his hands by a quarterback. He didn't release me until his cock finally softened enough to easily slip away from my sphincter's tight grip.

"They'll be back from church soon," Tony said.

"So?"

"So, what do we tell everybody?"

"We don't tell them anything," I said. "I'll be out of here in a few minutes and they won't even know I came back here with you." I began collecting my clothes.

"Will I see you again?"

"How can you avoid me now?"

That's when we decided that Tony needed a tutor, and who better than his come-to-Jesus buddy from Sunday school?

I've been tutoring Tony two or three nights a week ever since and, even though we don't actually study when we're together, his grades have actually improved. And his reputation as a campus stud, with female eye candy clinging to him at every frat party, remains intact.

Celebrity Crush

While other college students spent their weekends protesting Richard Nixon, the Vietnam War, and the university's dress code, I remained in the men's dorm lounge and watched creature feature marathons broadcast by a low-wattage UHF channel in the valley. At nine o'clock every Saturday evening Vlad Turnblatt hosted a triple-feature consisting of old black-and-white monster movies. He introduced each flick using a bad Romanian accent impaired by ill-fitting fangs, and he resurfaced during some of the commercial breaks to make bad jokes, pitch products, and promote local businesses.

Vlad wore his long dark hair slicked back, and his widow's peak was obviously painted on, as was his unnaturally pale skin tone. He wore a high-collared, full-length cape over a too-tight tuxedo with a white vest and white bowtie, and he most often appeared on camera rising from or standing in front of a coffin. Behind the coffin hung a dark curtain and at each end of the coffin stood a candelabrum. Each candelabrum held three white tapered candles, though the candles were never lit, and a lone spotlight appeared to illuminate the entire set. A single stationary camera captured Vlad's movements as long as he remained within its focal range, and part of a boom microphone often appeared at the top of the television screen when he was on-camera.

After the last movie, Vlad signed off with a message reminding viewers to beware of creatures that hide in the closet, followed by a clip of flying Navy jets played behind an all-instrumental rendition of "The Star-Spangled Banner." Then a test pattern filled the screen for a few minutes before the station's transmission ended and the screen turned to snow.

The black-and-white television in the dorm lounge was sufficient to watch old movies, but anything broadcast in color was lost to us; several months passed before I learned that the inside of Vlad's cape was red, that the curtain behind the coffin was a deep royal blue, and that everything else on Vlad or on the set was either black or white.

My roommate, Winchester Smith, thought I was a B-movie aficionado because I knew that *Gunsmoke*'s James Arness played The Thing in *The Thing from Another World* and that *Bullitt*'s Steve McQueen had his first leading role in *The Blob*—arcane knowledge I gleaned from paying attention to Vlad's movie

41

introductions—but I was less a fan of the flicks than I was of the host. I had become fixated on him, and when I masturbated to relieve the constant pressure that came from being a college-aged male, it wasn't buxom coeds or my dorm mates that I imagined servicing. It was Vlad.

The creature feature host consumed my thoughts and invaded my dreams until one Saturday night I decided I had to meet him. Winchester had smoked something that took him on a private trip, so I borrowed the keys to his Volkswagen Beetle and drove sixty miles into the valley in search of the UHF station that broadcast the creature features. I found it just off a two-lane state highway, miles from the nearest town, a squat, square concrete building surrounded by a gravel parking lot at the base of a transmission tower. The building had no windows and a single dim bulb burned above the entrance.

Until I arrived, the only car parked on the gravel lot was a red AMC Gremlin. I parked Winchester's Beetle at the edge of the lot, rolled down both front windows, and watched the windowless steel door until it opened thirty minutes later. Every time I had imagined that moment, I had expected Vlad to walk through the open doorway, his cape fluttering in the wind.

He didn't.

And there wasn't any wind.

The man who walked out of the UHF station wore faded Levi's and a suede fringe jacket over an untucked white undershirt. His black hair was still slicked back but the painted-on widow's peak had been wiped away, as had the makeup that made his skin appear pale on the television screen. He locked the steel door behind him and turned toward the Gremlin. He stopped when he saw the Volkswagen, and his right hand disappeared beneath the jacket as he reached around to the small of his back. The next time I saw his hand it was wrapped around the grip of a Saturday Night Special. He crunched across the gravel lot and shoved the revolver through the open car window until the barrel pressed against my forehead. "What are you going to do now, punk?"

"I'm going to crap my pants," I said.

He hesitated a moment and then withdrew the revolver. "You weren't planning to rob me?"

I shook my head. "No."

"Jesus, Kid, you should see the look on your face," he said as he tucked the revolver into his Levi's at the small of his back. "What are you doing here at this time of night?"

"I just wanted to meet Vlad Turnblatt."

"Big fan?"

"The biggest."

"Well, you've met him. Disappointed?"

"A little bit," I admitted.

Up close I realized that he wasn't much older than me, but he was bigger—taller and thick-chested, with muscular arms—and he was handsome in a rough-hewn way. His slicked-back hair reached to his collar. He hadn't quite removed all the makeup he'd worn as Vlad, and I could see flecks of white in his pores.

"Paul Foster." He shoved his hand through the window again and I shook it awkwardly. "When I'm not in costume."

"William Liskow," I said.

As Paul pulled back his hand, he asked, "Want to see the set, Kid?"

I did, and I said so.

"Come on."

I climbed out of Winchester's Volkswagen and followed Paul. He unlocked the steel door and led me into the station. As he showed me a couple of offices and a lot of equipment I didn't comprehend, he told me about the junkie who'd jumped him in the parking lot two weeks earlier and who, after a brief struggle, had given up the revolver, three doobies, and a baggie half-filled with unidentifiable pills. Paul said, "I flushed the pills, smoked two of the joints, and kept the gun to protect myself against anyone else who got the bright idea that I might be an easy mark out here in the middle of nowhere."

When he opened the last door and switched on the fluorescent lights, I finally saw the creature feature set in color. The reality was less impressive than it appeared on the television screen, and it had appeared low budget even in black-and-white. A camera and a spotlight had been placed in the middle of a large, square room painted institutional gray. Both could easily be pointed at any of three sets: The brightly colored Saturday morning children's show set on the west wall, the dark Saturday night creature feature set on the north wall, and the pulpit in front of the east wall from behind which a preacher of indeterminate faith led the sunrise Sunday morning religious program. Sometime after sign-off the candelabrums had been moved from the creature feature set to the sunrise Sunday morning set, and they bookended the pulpit. Pushed up against the south wall, which contained the door through which we had entered, were a makeup table and a metal rack where various costumes hung, including a tan three-piece suit for the preacher, a one-piece red-and-white clown costume with accompanying red fright wig, and Vlad Turnblatt's tuxedo and cape. I stroked the cape with my finger and unexpectedly felt my dick stir inside my jeans.

Paul noticed what I was doing. "You like that, Kid?"

That was the third time he'd called me "kid," even though he wasn't much older than me, and I asked why.

"How old are you?" he asked.

"Twenty."

"What do you do?"

"I'm a sophomore at State."

"Yeah," he said. "You're a kid. At your age I was shipping out to Vietnam. I saw a lot of stuff there, stuff nobody should have to see. I kept my mouth shut, got out before I could be kicked out, and came home to people spitting on me and calling me names. Shit like that'll age you, Kid."

Almost any of my dorm mates could have been among the spitters. We all had educational deferments, and the protest marches I avoided often included meeting returning soldiers at the airport and showering them with epithets and saliva, as if having tuition money somehow made us superior to the draftees.

While we spoke of Paul's military service, I continued fingering the cape, having captured the hem between my thumb and fingers. By then my dick stood fully erect and it strained at the confines of my jeans. If I'd been alone, I might have released it, wrapped it in the cloth of the cape, and pleasured myself. Instead, I asked, "Why did you say you got out of the Army before you could be kicked out?"

"Because I was never interested in the hoochie-mamas." Paul stared hard at me and waited for me to realize what the alternative might be. Then he reached out and trailed the backs of his fingers down my cheek, a move that sent an unexpected shiver of desire racing through my entire body. "You came all the way out here for a reason," he continued, "and it wasn't for me, was it? It was for Vlad."

I nodded.

"I can arrange that." Paul withdrew his fingers. Then he snatched Vlad's costume from the rack, tearing the cape from my grasp, and exited the room.

I glanced at the pulpit and at the children's show set, but neither interested me. I walked to the creature feature set at the far end of the room and examined the coffin, which seemed real enough. A pair of sawhorses held it aloft and a bit of royal blue drapery identical to that used as the backdrop had been attached to the bottom of the coffin as a skirt. A metal stepstool never visible on-camera allowed Vlad to climb into and out of the coffin.

When the overhead lights went dark, I turned and was momentarily blinded when the spotlight snapped on. I blinked and Vlad stepped into the light. Paul had pulled on the costume and had even reapplied his makeup, though not with the same precision as he did for the triple feature. His widow's peak was crooked, and the white greasepaint didn't quite cover his entire face. When he smiled, I saw the tips of his plastic fangs and then, using the bad Romanian accent I knew from watching the creature features, he said, "Do you vant me? I vant you."

He grabbed his cape with each hand and raised his arms, causing it to rise like bat wings as he swooped towards me. He wrapped his arms around me, completely engulfing me in the cape, and mashed his lips against mine as he forced his tongue into my mouth. Though I had imagined it often, I had never kissed a guy and my dick had never been harder than it was right then.

I surrendered to the moment.

The long, deep, rough kiss with Vlad's plastic fangs poking my lips and jabbing at my tongue stole my breath and made my knees weak. As we kissed, Vlad slid one hand between us and cupped the bulge in my jeans. His thick fingers stroked my erection through the material of my Levi's, and I moaned into his mouth.

He only teased me, though, and withdrew his hand so that he could guide one of my hands to the bulge in his pants. I could tell through the thin material of the tuxedo slacks that his dick was longer and thicker than mine, a supposition I confirmed when Vlad's hand on my shoulder urged me to my knees. He unzipped his fly and released the button at the waistband of his pants, and they slid to the floor to pool around his ankles. He wore nothing beneath the pants and his dick sprang free in front of my face.

I wrapped my hand around the stiff shaft and admired the swollen purple mushroom cap that pointed at my face. Unsure what to do, I looked up.

Vlad licked the tips of his fangs. "I vant you to suck"—he hesitated—"my dick." Then his hands on the back of my head as he pushed his dick forward made it clear what he wanted. I opened my mouth and wrapped my lips around his dick head, tasting him as I caressed it with my tongue. My hand pistoned up and down his stiff shaft.

Vlad began pulling his hips back and pushing forward, a little more of his dick sliding into my mouth with each forward thrust until I accepted his entire length. The dark tangle of his crotch hair tickled my nose and his heavy ball sac slapped against my chin.

And then he came, and I gagged on the sudden eruption of sexual effluent in my mouth. Even though his dick was still spasming, Vlad pulled away and I spit.

He looked down at me. "Your first time?"

I nodded.

Vlad had been satisfied, but it had done nothing for me, and my dick was still hard. While he stepped out of the tuxedo pants pooled around his feet, I sat on the stepstool and pulled off my hi-top basketball shoes, peeled out of my jeans, and dropped my BVDs to the floor.

When I stood, Vlad pressed against me from behind, wrapped his arms around me, and kissed my neck and my shoulder. He still wore the plastic fangs, and the points tickled my skin. His hands traveled down my chest and down my abdomen until he reached my crotch. He took my dick in one hand and jerked me off, his grip harder and his pistoning faster than my own when I stroked myself on so many Saturday nights after the UHF station signed off. I'd been primed by all that we'd done, and I came quickly, squirting come on the coffin skirt.

By then Vlad's dick had grown hard again and I felt it sandwiched between my ass cheeks. I leaned forward and braced myself on the stepstool as Vlad wiped some of the white greasepaint from his face and rubbed it on the tight pucker of my ass. He massaged it in until my sphincter loosened, and he could slip a finger into me. He wiped more greasepaint off his face and coated his dick with it. Then he pulled his finger out of me and pressed his dick head against the loosened hole. He eased into me, slowly sinking his entire length into my ass, drew back until only his dick head remained inside me, and then eased himself forward again. Again, he pulled back and pushed forward, a little harder and a little faster, and then again.

Then Vlad grabbed my hips and held me tight as he pounded into me. The stepstool wasn't stable enough for vigorous activity and it collapsed. Only Vlad's firm grip kept me from pitching to the floor with it, and then he slammed into me one last time and erupted within me.

After Vlad caught his breath, he pulled away. The next time I saw him he was Paul again, wearing his Levi's, white undershirt, and fringe jacket. By then I had also dressed. He walked me outside and locked the door behind us.

We sat on the hood of his Gremlin, and he lit a doobie, the last of the three he'd taken from the punk. We passed it back and forth until there wasn't enough left to hold, and Paul ate it.

"We cool, Kid?" he asked.

"We're cool."

I slid off the Gremlin, crossed the lot to Winchester's Volkswagen, and drove back to campus without looking back. My roommate woke when I returned his car keys to his desk, pushed himself up on one elbow, and looked at me from his bed. "What happened to you?"

I didn't know what he was talking about until I glanced in the mirror and saw white and black greasepaint smeared across my face. "Nothing you'd want to hear about," I told him. "Go back to sleep."

Even though I continued watching Vlad on the Saturday night triple feature, and even though I masturbated often while remembering that evening on the creature feature set, I never returned to the UHF station.

Several years later I had a crush on one of the members of Kiss—maybe it was the makeup—but I never pursued it. No more celebrity encounters for me. By then I had learned to appreciate real relationships, and the man I was with then and am still with now is perfectly willing to indulge my fantasies...even if they involve white greasepaint, plastic fangs, and a long, flowing cape.

Boys of Summer

I don't think any of us expected that Saturday to turn out the way it did, but with temperatures in the triple digits, a cooler filled with Shiner Bock in the bed of Delbert's Chevy Silverado, and the swimming hole all to ourselves, I don't see how it could have turned out any different.

The swimming hole is a wide spot in Carter Creek, on private property a mile and a half up a two-rut road from a Farm to Market. Delbert had a key to the gate, having done odd jobs for Old Man Carter, and it was his idea to be shed of town for the afternoon. He talked Gary and me into joining him when he offered to provide the beer and the ice to keep it cold.

We didn't plan ahead all that well and, when Delbert pulled his truck to a stop under the towering oak that shaded the near side of the swimming hole, we realized that not a one of us had brought swimming trunks and we only had towels because Delbert kept a supply in his toolbox to use as rags when he was working away from the house.

That didn't slow us down none. We just stripped down to our altogether and let our peckers flap in the wind as we waded into the cool, spring-fed creek. The ground on the near side, where we'd left the truck, was pretty near flat, sloping gradually into the water, and we could easily walk into the creek until we were about waist-deep before the bottom dropped away. Of course, by then, cold-water shrinkage had affected us all and none of our peckers were flapping. The creek's more than about ten feet deep on the far side, where it butts up against a rock wall about twenty feet high, and if we were of a mind to, we could climb about five feet up that cliff and cannonball into the water below. Delbert, being the more adventurous of us, did it three times before an accidental belly flop had him yelping in pain and had Gary and me laughing our butts off. After that we just swam and floated and shot the breeze.

All three of us had farmer's tans—leather-brown faces, red necks, and dark arms from our fingertips to the leading edge of our T-shirt sleeves. Except for various amounts of body hair, everything else about us was albino white and when any one of us headed to the Silverado for beer we looked like ghosts emerging from the water.

After a few beers we started horsing around. Delbert dunked Gary. Gary dunked me. I dunked Gary again. And soon our excitement counteracted the cold-water shrinkage we'd experienced earlier.

We had been friends forever, the three of us, and we'd paired off a few times over the years, but that afternoon was the first time the three of us ever did anything together.

It started when Delbert and me spotted Gary floating on his back with his eyes closed and his pecker standing at full attention. Now Gary's not what you'd call a longhorn, but his erect pecker cast a nice enough shadow, nonetheless.

Delbert nudged me and then dove under the water. He came up on the other side of Gary and grabbed a fistful of Gary's pecker just as I came up under Gary and supported his ass to prevent him from sinking or pulling away.

"What're you dreamin' about, some skinny-ass city boy down in Austin?"

Gary protested at first, but when Delbert started pistoning his fist up and down the length of Gary's pecker shaft, the swollen purple mushroom cap popping out the top of Delbert's fist like a one-eyed prairie dog, Gary quit struggling and was soon moving his hips in rhythm to Delbert's fist pumps.

I couldn't help myself. While Delbert jerked off Gary, my own pecker grew stiff as a fence post, and I knew I was going to have to do something to relieve the pressure. Though tempted to reach under the water and take matters into my own hands, I continued supporting Gary's weight until he came.

He erupted like a geyser, jetting a long, thin stream of come straight up in the air that rained down on his chest. Delbert released his grip on Gary's pecker, and I pushed him away, sending him floating toward deep water as he tried to catch his breath and keep from sinking at the same time.

I walked out of the water to Delbert's Silverado, my erect pecker leading the way, and grabbed a fresh bottle of Shiner Bock from the cooler resting on the open tailgate.

"You're going to get a sunburn on that thing," Delbert called.

"Not if I find a dark place to stick it," I called back. I popped open the beer and took a long swallow.

"We ain't got any lube," Gary protested as he left the water to join me.

"In my glove box, dumb ass," Delbert shouted from the creek. "You think I go anywhere without it?"

After Gary opened his own Shiner Bock, he walked around the truck to the passenger side and retrieved a half-used tube of lube from the glove box. He tossed it to me. I fumbled a one-handed catch because the tube was hot, and it dropped onto the tailgate.

"We ain't going to be using this any time soon," I said as I picked up the lube with two fingers and dropped it into the beer cooler. "Use this now it'll be like dipping your pecker in French fry grease."

Then I spread one of Delbert's crusty towels on the tailgate so I wouldn't burn my bare ass and hiked myself onto it. My pecker was still jutting up from my crotch like some kind of petrified snake, and Gary noticed it when he returned to my side.

"What are you planning to do with that?" he asked.

"I was planning to do you," I said, "until I burned my fingers on that tube of lube you threw at me."

"Maybe there's something we can do about it while we're waiting for the lube to chill."

"You suggesting what I think you're suggesting?"

Gary took a swallow of Shiner Bock and then wrapped his lips around my swollen pecker head. The combination of his hot lips and the cold beer made my eyes open wide.

"Jesus, Gary," I said to the back of his head. "Where'n hell did you ever get the idea to do that?"

I didn't expect a response and I didn't get one. Gary was too busy giving my pecker head a tongue lashing to say much of anything.

He wrapped one hand around my stiff shaft and began pumping up and down as he continued licking my pecker head. I set my beer aside and pressed my fingers against the back of his head. The bristly hair from his recent flattop jabbed my fingers like tiny cactus needles as I pressed down, encouraging Gary to take more than just my pecker head into his mouth.

He had to swallow the Shiner to do that, and he must have because he slowly took in my entire length. I soon felt his warm breath against my damp crotch hair, when Gary drew his face away from my crotch. His beer-wet lips slid smoothly up my pecker shaft. Then they slid back down. As I set my own beer aside, I glanced out at the creek. Delbert was watching us and, from the way the water was moving in front of him, I suspected he had taken matters into his own hands.

I leaned back and braced myself in the pickup bed as Gary face-fucked me. As far as I could see through the branches of the oak, there wasn't a cloud in the pale blue sky. But I only had a moment to notice. As my climax approached, I closed my eyes and felt my entire body begin to tense. Gary must have noticed because he reached between my thighs and grabbed my nut sac.

I couldn't restrain myself, even if I'd wanted to, and I erupted in Gary's mouth, providing him with a come chaser to his beer. My pecker spasmed several times and Gary swallowed every drop of my come.

My pecker quickly withered, and Gary pulled away. He retrieved his half-empty bottle of Shiner Bock, drained it, and ran back to the creek. As soon as I caught my breath, I rejoined Delbert and Gary in the water, and this time our horsing around involved more groping than roughhousing. Before long, our peckers had become fence posts again.

I caught Gary from behind when he was thigh deep in the water, bent over to look at something, and I shoved my erect pecker between his ass cheeks.

He pulled away. "Jesus, Carl, lube!"

"I'll bet it's cooled off my now."

He glanced back at me and then ran toward shore. I took off after him and passed him when we reached dry land. I reached the cooler first and fished out the tube of lube. It hadn't just cooled down; it was cold. I experienced a little involuntarily shrinkage when I first applied it to my pecker.

Gary had reached me by then and I spun him around, bent him over the tailgate, slathered some lube into his ass crack, and again slipped my pecker between his cheeks. He was tight, but I grabbed his hips and pressed forward. His resistance lasted only a moment and then my pecker head slid deep inside him.

I drew back and plunged forward, then did it again. Because I was concentrating on boning Gary and wasn't paying any attention to what Delbert was doing, I didn't see him rise from the creek and approach us from behind. I was surprised when I drew back and felt Delbert grab my hips and shove his pecker between my ass checks. He'd obviously lubed it up because it was slicker than snot, and when I shoved forward, he shoved forward, burying his pecker in my ass at the same time I buried mine in Gary's.

I've never been sandwiched before, and it was unlike anything I'd ever felt. We quickly found a rhythm, with me doing most of the work. As I drove into Gary, I pulled away from Delbert, and when I pulled back from Gary, I impaled myself on Delbert.

Gary had one hand braced on the tailgate and used his free hand to stroke his pecker, beating like he was trying to whip up a meringue. He came first, spraying come across the ground beneath the Silverado, and I came a moment later, emptying myself inside Gary with a grunt. I collapsed against him, pining him to the tailgate.

Delbert wasn't so easily satisfied. He took a half step forward as I leaned against Gary and continued drilling into me, pounding harder and faster until he slammed into me one last time and erupted within me.

Then his weight as he collapsed against my back kept Gary and me trapped until Gary complained. "Hey, guys, you're crushing me."

Delbert finally pulled away, and then I followed.

I fished three Shiner Bocks from the cooler and passed them around. Then we stood in a rough circle, our peckers dripping come and lube, and drank until we'd slaked our thirst.

None of us felt like swimming after that so we cleaned up, pulled on our clothes, and headed back to town. Delbert dropped Gary off at his apartment and then dropped me off at my house.

Although I didn't realize it until that evening, I was sunburned in places that don't usually see sun, and it was several weeks before any of us could stand a slap on the back or a slap on the ass without wincing.

I know because we kept slapping each other just to see who would complain the loudest.

Summer Folk

We went to the beach every summer whether we wanted to or not, and we stayed in a six-bedroom beach house with an ever-changing number of relatives. The boys shared one bedroom, the girls shared another, and our parents paired off into the other four bedrooms. The general overseer for the summer—my grandmother all the years I was growing up—had an efficiency apartment above the two-car garage. Our extended family lived in the house from Memorial Day weekend until Labor Day weekend, and when and how long each family stayed depended on a variety of factors often involving available vacation time and who had insulted whom over the Christmas holidays.

When I was young, I enjoyed spending several weeks at the beach with my cousins. As a teenager I resented mandatory fun in the sun when what I most craved was to lock myself in my bedroom, smoke pot, and fantasize about some of the guys in my gym class. During college, I skipped summers at the beach because I was working or enrolled in summer classes, but I had no job prospects when I graduated as an English major in the middle of a recession, and my mother convinced me to spend the entire summer at the house to act as general overseer, a responsibility my grandmother had tired of, and no other relative had stepped forward to accept.

My duties were minimal: manage the summer finances, keep the fridge stocked with staples, ensure that we never ran out of toilet paper, and call the appropriate repairman if the plumbing stopped up or one of the children threw a baseball through the front window. In exchange, I would live rent-free in the efficiency apartment above the garage for more than three months while I continued my job search by applying for positions I found online.

The house was empty when I arrived the Thursday preceding Memorial Day weekend, and I walked through the place with the caretaker, a local man who lived in town and took care of the property three seasons out of four. Charlie had already uncovered all the furniture, washed all the windows, and otherwise prepared the house for my family's arrival. I had not seen him in several years and was surprised at how slowly he moved and how much trouble he had climbing stairs to the second floor. After I saw that everything was in order, I followed Charlie's rattletrap pickup truck a mile north into town to stock up on the things we needed to start the summer.

I had a shopping list handed down by my grandmother; purchasing everything on the list filled two carts. A woman as old as the town rang up my purchases and an attractive blond man near my age bagged everything. He wore tight-fitting jeans and a torso-hugging polo shirt with the store's logo embroidered on one side of his chest and a name badge reading "Tony" pinned to the other. He bagged quickly and efficiently, hesitating every fifth item or so to brush a wayward lock of blond hair away from his pale blue eyes.

"Need help getting all this out?" he asked.

I did and I told him so.

As we pushed the carts out of the store, Tony said, "Looks like you're preparing for an invasion."

I laughed. "My family has a summer house south of town. I'm the advance guard."

"You're summer folk?"

"Most of my life," I said as we loaded everything into my car. "Haven't made it the past few years, though."

He looked me up and down as if taking my measure as a man, but I couldn't tell from his expression what his assessment might be. Then we both reached for my car's trunk to close it and his hand covered mine. An electric tingle shot up my arm, coursed through my entire body, and caused a tightening in my crotch. I took a deep breath. "Bag boy" wasn't on my grandmother's shopping list so, no matter how appealing I found Tony, he was a seductive treat best left at the grocery store. I said, "I have to go."

We closed the trunk together and Tony stepped away.

There wasn't much else to say, so I climbed behind the wheel of my Mustang and watched Tony's jeans-clad ass as he wheeled the two carts back into the store.

* * *

I saw Tony jogging along the beach early the next morning. He wore neon-blue running shorts, white running shoes covered with clinging wet sand, and nothing else, revealing the long, lean body of a swimmer. Even though it was an unusually warm May morning on the Jersey shore, it was too cold for me to be outside without my full-length terrycloth robe wrapped around me, and I was sitting on the deck of the main house drinking coffee, enjoying my last morning of solitude before my relatives invaded. Tony saw me watching him and waved.

I called to him. "I have a fresh pot of coffee and a spare cup. You interested?"

He crossed the beach and climbed the steps. By the time he reached the deck, I had ducked into the house, retrieved a cup, and was filling it with coffee from the thermal carafe. As he settled into the deck chair next to me, his pebbled skin, tight areolas, and firm nipples revealed that he was colder than he let on and probably needed the coffee. I asked, "Cream? Sugar?"

"Black's fine."

I handed him the cup and he sipped from it. Then he glanced over his shoulder at the house. "This your place?"

The house had been in my family for several generations, owned and maintained by a family trust overseen by a board of directors made up of family members. I said, "It's as much mine as anyone else's."

He brushed a long lock of blond hair away from his eyes. "Must be nice."

"How's that?"

"To have a place like this to spend your summers," he said. "I've lived up the coast my entire life, but never in a place like this."

Tony and I had probably crossed paths when we were younger, but we never would have played together. Children of the locals and the summer folk intermingled only by accident. Now that we were older, our differences seemed less significant and the vibe I felt from his proximity suggested we had more in common than expected. For a moment I imagined what it might be like to lick the sweat off his chest, drum my fingers on his abdominal six-pack, or rest my hand on his muscular thigh prior to intermingling with him. My thoughts made my robe tent beneath the table, and I leaned forward.

Just as I convinced myself to place my hand on Tony's forearm to see his reaction, he finished his coffee and placed the empty cup on the serving tray next to the carafe. As he stood, he said, "Thanks for this."

"Anytime," I told him. "You're welcome anytime."

His gaze wandered over me, taking in my tousled bed hair and tightly fastened robe. "If you're ever in town some evening," he said, "come by the Dew Drop Inn. I usually stop there after work."

"I will," I promised, though I wasn't yet certain it was a promise I would keep. He took the steps two at a time down to the beach and continued jogging south, away from town. I watched him until I ran out of coffee. By then he was barely a speck in the distance.

* * *

My relatives started arriving early that evening, beginning with my mother's oldest brother and his second wife. By the time the sun set Saturday evening, the house was filled with family members, including my parents and grandmother, representing all generations and various degrees of separation. The house was ready for their arrival, but I wasn't. I had forgotten how loud a houseful of my relatives could be, and I was glad to disappear into the garage apartment each evening.

Memorial Day meant hot dogs grilled on the beach, tubs of potato salad, and pots of baked beans. The children drank gallons of pop, and the adults worked their way through several bottles of wine and a few cases of beer, some starting as early as breakfast with mimosas on the deck. By the time the sun went down the questions began.

Most of them hadn't seen me in four years and they wanted to know everything about my life. I answered the questions I could, deflected the questions I didn't wish to answer, and did my best to avoid the nosiest among them.

By Wednesday I'd had enough of my relatives and even my private apartment over the garage was too close to them. I drove up the coast to town and found the Dew Drop Inn, a waterfront watering hole that catered to locals. I saw more plaid wool shirts than polo shirts and more work boots than penny loafers, so I knew as I crossed to the bar that I didn't fit in. I knew enough to order a beer rather than a mixed drink, and I carried my bottle to an empty booth where I could sit and watch the door.

I'd been there about twenty minutes and was well into my second beer before Tony arrived. He wore his work clothes but had removed his name badge. He ordered a beer and came to my table.

"Slumming?" he asked as he slid into the booth opposite me.

"Avoiding my family," I explained. "My grandmother wants to know when I'm planning to settle down with a nice girl and my mother wants to know when she'll have grandchildren."

He hesitated with his beer halfway to his lips. "You haven't told them?"

"Not yet."

"So, summer folk have the same problems as the rest of us?"

I knew at that moment that we were speaking the same coded language. "You haven't told your family, either?"

"Nope." He lifted the beer the rest of the way to his lips and drained half the bottle.

I glanced around the bar and wondered what he did for companionship in a town small enough that everyone likely knew everyone else's business. I had finished my second beer by then and he had almost finished his first. I asked, "You want another?"

"Let's get out of here," he suggested. "I have beer in the fridge at home."

* * *

Home turned out to be a cottage on the inland side of town. We both parked in the driveway because a Jet Ski occupied the one-car garage; I had to step around a pair of body boards on the porch to reach the back door.

"Spend a lot of time in the water?" I asked as Tony pushed open the door and led me into the kitchen.

"On it, in it, or near it," he said.

The kitchen had been completely renovated, and Tony pulled two bottles of beer from the stainless-steel refrigerator. He opened both and handed one to me.

I put my bottle on the granite counter. "This isn't why we're here, is it?"

He shook his head and placed his beer next to mine, sweat from the bottles intermingling on the countertop. Months had passed since my last sexual encounter, and I had never been with a man I knew so little about.

Nervous, I pushed blond hair away from his blue eyes and then covered his lips with mine. Our kiss was long and deep, and we were tugging at each other's clothes long before it ended.

After I peeled off his shirt, I kissed my way down his neck to his deeply tanned, hairless chest, pausing to suckle each of his nipples before dropping to my knees and unfastening his jeans. As I pulled his jeans and his boxers to his knees and let them drop to his ankles, Tony's thick cock sprang free of the confining material.

His cock was as pale as the rest of his skin from his waist to his thighs, evidence that he spent a good deal of time in nothing but running shorts and swimming trunks, and it throbbed in front of my face. I wrapped my fist around the base of his shaft and licked away a glistening drop of pre-come before I took the spongy soft helmet head into my mouth. As I licked his cock head, I pistoned my fist up and down the stiff shaft.

Tony held the back of my head, applying pressure that let me know he wanted me to take in more of his cock. I had not had a cock in my mouth since the New Year's Eve party at my frat house, so I took it in slowly, licking and sucking and licking more as it filled my oral cavity.

When I had taken in as much as I could, I pulled back and then did it again. I cupped Tony's sac with my free hand, massaging his balls as I stroked the delicate area between his sac and his ass with the tip of one finger.

Apparently, I was moving too slow for Tony. As he held my head, he drew back his hips and pushed forward, driving his cock in and out of my mouth until he could restrain himself no longer. With one last thrust, he came, firing a thick wad of hot spunk against the back of my throat.

I didn't swallow because I never swallow. When his cock quit spasming, I stood and kissed Tony again, surprising him with a mouthful of his own come. He pushed me away, spit into the sink, and quickly rinsed his mouth with a swallow of beer.

"That was a surprise," Tony said. "Nobody around here does that."

He pulled off his shoes and stepped out of his jeans and boxers. He helped me out of my clothes and then bent me over the island. I grabbed hold of the granite countertop as he spread my legs and stepped between them. He dribbled olive oil down my ass crack until it dripped from my ball sac and then he slid his middle finger down my crack until it was slick with olive oil.

He pressed the tip of his slickened finger against my ass hole until my sphincter opened to admit it. His erection had returned and a moment later he pulled his finger free and replaced it with his cock head. Then he grabbed my hips and pushed his entire length deep inside me.

My own cock was hard, and I wrapped my fist around it. As Tony pounded into me from behind, I stroked my cock. The faster he pumped, the faster I pumped. I came first, firing my load against the underside of the granite countertop, but Tony continued pounding into me for another dozen strokes until he couldn't restrain himself and he came with one final, powerful thrust.

He stood behind me, holding my hips as his cock throbbed inside my ass. He asked, "You have a name?"

"Chad."

After he pulled away, we dressed and drank our beers.

Then I left, wondering all the way back to my family's beach house if I had been too easy and if I would see Tony again.

* * *

But that wasn't the end of things. On the mornings when I woke early enough and took my coffee on the deck, I would see Tony jogging south along the beach. Most mornings he wore gray sweats, no longer seeking to seduce me with his toned body. We waved, but he never approached while my family was present.

On those evenings when I tired of the never-ending parade of noisy relatives who moved in and out of the beach house during the summer, I drove myself to the Dew Drop Inn, shared a beer with Tony, and then followed him to his cottage.

By mid-July we stopped all pretense of running into one another at the inn and I drove directly to his place on those evenings when I tired of my extended family and desired his physical attention. We spent hours in Tony's bed. He taught me the value of a steady relationship, something I'd never really had in college. On his days off from the grocery store, Tony took me out on his Jet Ski, and he taught me how to body board at the beach north of town.

By the time our summer romance was half over, it was obvious neither of us wanted it to end—yet neither of us would broach the subject directly. We were trying to milk every moment of passion we could from our remaining time together.

"Summer folk always leave," Tony said one night as I was dressing to return to my family's beach house. He lay on his bed, still naked and sweaty from our earlier entanglement.

I pulled my shirt into place and tucked it into my chinos. "What if they didn't?"

"I've lived here my entire life, Chad. Summer folk always leave. That's just the way it is." He turned away, unwilling to hear me deny the truth we both knew.

* * *

One afternoon near the end of August, our caretaker's wife called to tell us Charlie had suffered a heart attack and was in the hospital.

"It doesn't look good," she said. "Even if he survives this, he won't be able to continue working."

My grandmother led a troop of older family members—those who had known Charlie for several decades—to the hospital. When they returned, my grandmother chaired a meeting of the family members present at the beach house and updated us all on his status. Labor Day weekend was rapidly approaching, and we had limited time to find a replacement.

After more than an hour of discussion, I said, "I'll do it."

Every adult in the room turned to look at me. No member of the family had ever served as caretaker for the beach house, just as no member of the family had ever lived year-round on the property.

"You'll have to commit to the entire year," my grandmother said.

I knew what Charlie had been paid. Though not much, when combined with rent-free living in the garage apartment, I could scrape by. I could maybe find a part-time job in town for extra spending money or spend my time applying to graduate school. My only other option was to boomerang back to my bedroom in my parents' house because I hadn't done any online job hunting since the night I'd first met Tony at the Dew Drop Inn. I said, "That's not a problem."

The adults talked for another hour, came up with no better solution, and finally offered me the position.

The next night, while reclining on Tony's bed watching him undress, I told him I would be remaining at the beach house after Labor Day.

He turned. "How long?"

"At least until next summer." As he settled onto the bed next to me, I told him what had happened.

"This changes everything," Tony said when I finished.

"I know," I said. "Summer folk don't always leave."

He stared deep into my eyes, placed his hands on either side of my head, and kissed me—softly, tenderly, his lips lingering as if we had all the time in the world. Then he caressed me, letting his fingers explore every inch of my body before I turned my back to him. I handed him the nearly empty tube of lube from his nightstand and soon he entered me.

We made love—slow, sweet love, unlike all the times before when our sex had been hard and fast and without commitment—and I fell asleep in Tony's arms. For the first time since we'd met, I spent the night, slipping back into the garage apartment at the beach house moments before dawn. I'd barely been home five minutes when I heard someone climbing the steps.

I opened the apartment door just as my grandmother reached the little deck that served as a porch.

"You think nobody knows," she said, "but we do. Some of us. You be careful. You don't let this local boy break your heart."

I smiled. "I won't, Grandma. I'll be careful."

"And if he does, you let me know. I'm sure we can find someone to watch the house if you need to leave."

"I'll be okay."

She patted my arm. "So, you clean up and then come over to the house. I'm fixing pancakes this morning, and I need your help."

* * *

My relatives started heading home on Saturday, just as noisy in their departures as they were in their arrivals. The last to leave—a second cousin and her family—drove away mid-afternoon on Labor Day. The next morning, I had the entire place to myself. I woke early, made coffee, and sat on the deck awaiting Tony's arrival.

Our summer romance was over. Now it was time to see what the future really held.

Creosote Flats and the Big Spread

West Texas creosote flats are covered with little more than creosote bush, yucca, and cholla cactus, and they stretch for miles in every direction. I know this because I traveled through the middle of a creosote flat for several hours after following my GPS system's instructions to turn off the main road and take a more direct route to my destination just across the New Mexico border.

The paved road gave way to gravel. Gravel gave way to dirt. Soon there wasn't much of a road at all. That's when my GPS system stopped working, my radiator blew fluid all over the engine, and I found myself standing alongside my overheated hybrid unable to get a signal on my iPhone.

Dressed for comfort, I wore penny loafers without socks, olive green cargo shorts, and a khaki polo shirt. I'd spent the previous day at the salon, where I'd had my hair styled and my eyebrows sugared. I looked fabulous, but fabulous wouldn't last long without air conditioning. I hadn't brought a change of clothes and I hadn't thought to pack a hat.

I stared back in the direction I had come, knowing the main road was far behind me, and stared up the road in the direction I had been going, seeing the hard-packed dirt degrade into two parallel ruts. None of my three choices—go back, go forward, or remain where I was—appealed to me, and triple-digit heat did not enhance my decision-making ability.

After finishing the diet Dr Pepper I'd been nursing since lunch, I fashioned a head covering out of some napkins and a box from the chicken takeout place where I had stopped, doing my best to imitate the headgear worn by Foreign Legionnaires in all the old movies I watched with my father on Saturday afternoons. Then I began walking back the way I had come, hoping that a known destination was better than the unknown and that I would soon reach a point where my iPhone would pick up a signal.

Less than an hour later, I had blisters on both heels, the napkins covering my ears had begun to shred, and the musky citrus scent of the expensive aftershave I'd dabbed on that morning had been replaced by the overpowering stench of chicken grease. I stopped and tried my iPhone but still couldn't get a signal. I cursed my GPS system, my iPhone, and myself for being so reliant on technology that I hadn't prepared for the Texas that exists beyond the Austin city limits.

I had just started walking again when I heard a vaguely familiar sound behind me, a clip-clop I associated with old John Wayne movies. I spun around and found myself staring up into the deeply tanned face of a mouth-wateringly handsome cowboy astride a white mare. He must have been ten years my senior, wore a white Stetson with a low crown and wide brim over finger-length salt-and-pepper hair, a red bandanna tied loosely around his neck, a long-sleeve white shirt under a tan wool vest, faded Wrangler jeans under leather chaps, and well-worn Justin boots with silver spurs. Clearly, I amused him—standing there in my dusty city clothes, wearing a chicken box for a hat—because the cowboy's pale blue eyes sparkled and the corners of his lips were pulled up in a grin I felt certain he was trying his best to suppress. He touched his index finger to the brim of his Stetson. "Afternoon."

"Afternoon," I replied.

"Where you headed?" he asked.

"Back where I came from."

"Where's that?'

"Austin."

"Long walk, ain't it?"

I held up my iPhone. "I was just planning to walk until I could get a signal on this."

He jerked a thumb over his shoulder. "That your car back there?"

I told him it was. I returned my iPhone to one pocket of my cargo shorts and resealed the Velcro flap.

"Where were you headed?"

"New Mexico."

"And why did you come this way?"

I told him about following the instructions of my GPS system and his suppressed grin turned into a full-throated laugh.

"Lucky I found you," he said, "before the coyotes and the buzzards picked your carcass clean."

I shuddered.

The cowboy held out his hand. "Get on up here and I'll carry you back to the house."

As I reached out, he grasped my wrist, so I grasped his. Then he jerked me into the air like I weighed nothing at all and dropped me into the saddle behind him. The last horse I'd ridden was plugged into the front of a Safeway grocery store and cost my mother a quarter. Because I had no idea what I should do, I wrapped my arms around the cowboy's broad chest. He removed my hands from his chest and placed them on the saddle horn. Then I held on tight as he guided the mare off the road and through the creosote bush, yucca, and cholla cactus.

"What's your name?" I asked.

"Carl Rogers," he said over his shoulder. "My friends call me 'Buck.'"

It was my turn to suppress a grin.

"You?"

"Stephen Chambers," I told him. "My friends don't call often enough."

As we rode uphill, I quickly learned to appreciate Buck's leather chaps, and I tucked my bare legs as close behind his legs as I could to protect them from the cactus and other flora intent on filleting my shins. The mare's gentle gait and Buck's up-and-down movement caused his tight ass to rub against my crotch, causing a physical reaction I did not, at that time, appreciate. If Buck noticed my saddle horn jabbing into his backside, he was polite enough not to mention it.

When we crested the hill, I looked down at a compound that included a massive adobe-and-stone ranch house with a satellite dish beside it, a multi-car garage with a small, single-prop airplane parked behind it, a barn with a corral containing two horses, and a pair of smaller buildings—one covered with solar panels—I didn't recognize. In the far distance I saw oil wells and longhorn cattle.

"Your place?" I asked.

"One of them."

I considered Buck's response as the mare made its way downhill and into the barn where we dismounted. Buck removed the horse's saddle and other tack, brushed it quickly, and then led it into the corral with the other horses. The mare promptly stuck its face in the water trough.

Buck clapped a big hand on my shoulder. "You look a mite parched," he said. "Let's head up to the house and see if we can quench your thirst."

He led me across the compound, through the back door, and into a kitchen that was a chef's stainless-steel wet dream bigger than my entire Austin apartment. As I walked toward the sink, one of Buck's big paws lifted the chicken box from my head and dropped it into a waste can. Then he removed his Stetson and placed it on the counter before opening the refrigerator and offering me a selection of bottled beverages.

After I chose Shiner Bock, my host pulled out two bottles, opened one, and handed it to me. He opened the other bottle, downed most of it in one long swallow, and finished it before I had taken more than a couple of sips from mine. He tossed the empty on top of my chicken-box hat and pulled another bottle from the fridge. Then he offered to show me the place.

Buck had furnished the ranch house in Texas chic—white limestone accent walls, oversized furniture with a Spanish influence, plenty of leather and cowhide, Texas Star drawer pulls—and many of the rooms appeared as if they had been set-designed as King Ranch catalog pages and were awaiting arrival of the photographer. The den, a room where Buck obviously spent much of his time, sported a wall-mounted big-screen television at one end, and overflowing floor-to-ceiling bookshelves covered the other three walls. A well-worn leather couch in the center of the room faced the television, and a paperback mystery, its spine broken, lay open and facedown on one cushion. A colorful Mexican serape blanket lay in a wad on the other cushion, as if whoever had been using it had tossed it aside before rising.

The only other rooms that appeared lived-in were the master bedroom and master bathroom upstairs. The unmade king-size hacienda bed with headboard and footboard wrapped in nutmeg-colored leather dominated Buck's bedroom, and French doors on the east side of the room opposite the bed opened onto a broad porch. A stack of magazines littered one nightstand, a pile of laundry—apparently clean and waiting to be folded and put away—covered a leather sleeper chair.

When I followed Buck down the back stairs and into his office, the phone on the corner of his massive oak desk reminded me that I still hadn't contacted anyone about my disabled vehicle. I dug my iPhone from my pocket, checked it, and realized I still had no signal. I looked up at my host. "I need to contact someone about my car."

Buck picked up his desk phone and was soon giving the GPS coordinates of my abandoned hybrid to someone on the other end of the conversation.

After the conversation ended and Buck replaced the handset in its cradle, I asked, "You have a landline all the way out here?"

"Satellite phone," he explained. "Costs a pretty penny, but worth every cent."

"And my car?"

"My mechanic will pick it up in the morning and let us know what it needs as soon as he can work it in."

"What'll I do until then?"

He hesitated and I waited through the silence.

"Spend the night," he suggested. "Or, if you want, I can take you to town, drop you off at the roach motel."

Was the handsome cowboy hitting on me?

"A man gets lonely out here by himself," Buck said as we returned to the kitchen to replace our empty Shiner Bocks. His gaze slid over me in a way that could easily be misunderstood. "You can only read so many books and watch so many movies before you start craving a little human contact."

He *was* hitting on me. I looked up into his sparkling blue eyes and felt certain I could get lost in there.

Before I could respond, Buck continued. "You smell like fried chicken and it's making me hungry," he said. "Why don't you go upstairs and take a shower? While you do that, I'll throw something on the grill for dinner."

He told me where to find towels and washcloths, and a few minutes later I was in the master bathroom stripping off my sweat-stained and chicken-scented clothing. The shower was as big as my entire bathroom, lined on the floor and three sides with glazed Mexican tile. A clear glass wall with a door in the middle constituted the fourth side.

After showering, I used antiseptic from the medicine cabinet for the scratches on my legs, splashed on some cologne from a bottle on the counter, and poked through the pile of clean laundry on the sleeper chair until I discovered gray drawstring sweatpants and a white T-shirt. Both were too big for me, but I made do.

I found Buck on the back patio, standing over a propane grill covered with foil-wrapped ears of corn and T-bones thick as decks of playing cards. When he saw me, he flipped the steaks onto plates, stacked the corn on a third plate, and carried everything to a picnic table where silverware, steak sauce, sticks of butter, and cold bottles of Shiner Bock waited.

"Good thing you're not one of those vegans," he said. "This is the best I could do on short notice."

"Don't worry," I told him as I stared into his eyes, "I enjoy a big piece of meat."

The grin I'd first seen when Buck found me earlier that day returned. He said, "I think we'll get along just fine."

I jabbed a knife into my steak, finding it charred on the outside and barely warm in the middle. Then I unwrapped an ear of corn, slathered it with butter, and began eating.

"So, what were you aiming to do in New Mexico when you got there?" Buck asked.

"Housewarming. A former roommate and his current squeeze bought a place together."

"Shouldn't you call and let then know you won't be there?"

"I don't think they'll miss me," I said, but I didn't tell Buck why. I hadn't been invited to the housewarming and had awoken that morning intent on crashing the party and making a scene in some lame attempt to convince my former roommate that he was making a mistake. That's why I hadn't bothered to pack, was relying on my GPS system to get me to a place I'd never been, and wasn't prepared when my hybrid overheated in the middle of a creosote flat. Which reminded me: "How did you find me?"

"Wasn't hard," Buck said around a mouthful of steak. "You'd been kicking up a rooster tail for hours. When the dust settled, I knew something had to be wrong, so I went for a look-see and there you were."

We talked about other things, including my job managing a used bookstore and lack of romantic prospects, and Buck told me about his inability to find his soul mate.

"I can buy companionship," he said, "but I can't buy love. That's why I spend most of my time here instead of the house in Aspen. In Aspen everybody's after my money. The only people likely to come out here would have to be interested in me."

"You believe in destiny?" I asked.

"How's that?"

"Maybe there was a reason my GPS system put me on the road to nowhere," I said, "because that road led me here, to you."

Buck smiled and lifted his bottle of Shiner Bock in toast. When I clinked my bottle against his, he said, "To destiny."

After dinner, I helped my host clean up. Then Buck went to the barn to tend to the horses while I nosed around his den. I found several first-edition mystery novels, many of the literary classics I'd been forced to read in high school and college, and a variety of business books. From the plethora of cracked spines, I knew the books weren't just for display. I appreciated that. Other than the bookstore customers—none of whom were in my social circle—I didn't know anyone who read as much as I did.

I was thumbing through the paperback Buck had left facedown on the leather couch—a collection of mystery short stories—when he returned from the barn. "I must smell a bit horsy," Buck said. "I'm headed upstairs for a shower."

After waiting several minutes, I followed my host. I slipped into the master bathroom, leaned back against the sink, and watched Buck through the glass wall of the shower. He was washing his salt-and-pepper hair, his eyes closed to keep out the shampoo, and I had time to really take him in. He had a cowboy tan; his face and arms were darkened and weathered, but the rest of his well-muscled body had not been exposed to the sun in several years.

Shampoo ran down Buck's powerful chest, and my gaze followed it over his six-pack abs, through the dark thatch of his pubic hair, and down the length of his thick phallus. I won't say he was hung like a horse, but I'm certain more than a few ponies would be jealous of what I saw dangling between Buck's thighs. I know it took my breath away.

Buck must have heard my intake of breath because he opened his eyes and looked at me through the glass. "I didn't hear you come in."

"I hope you don't mind."

"I don't have anything to hide." He squirted liquid soap on a washcloth and scrubbed his face, working his way down his torso to his legs. He straightened and returned his attention to the junction of his thighs and lathered up his pubic hair, causing his heavy ball sac to bounce up and down. Then he pulled back his foreskin and washed the head of his cock before washing the length of his stiffening shaft.

My own cock reacted to the sight and soon tented the front of the oversized sweatpants I'd pulled on after my shower earlier. I wet my lips with the tip of my tongue.

Buck cut off the water, reached out for a towel, and began drying himself. When he finished, he slung the towel around his shoulders and stepped from the shower stall.

I couldn't resist. I dropped to my knees on the bathroom floor, my face only inches from his fat phallus. When Buck didn't stop me, I wrapped my fist around his cock, pulled back his foreskin, and took the mushroom cap of his cock into my mouth. I painted his cock head with my tongue, tasting floral-scented soap as his cock stiffened, and then I slowly took his entire length into my mouth until his damp pubic hair tickled my nose, almost gagging because his cock was bigger than any I'd ever had before. I drew back and did it again.

As I cupped his heavy ball sac in my palm, I kneaded his nuts. With the tip of one finger, I stroked the sensitive spot behind his scrotum, and before long Buck couldn't restrain himself. He wrapped his thick fingers around the back of my head and face-fucked me, driving his thick cock in and out of my mouth, his balls bouncing against my chin. I grabbed his muscular thighs and felt him tense just before he came, so I was ready for the flood of warm come he fired against the back of my throat, and I swallowed again and again and held his slowly deflating cock in my mouth until I had licked away the last drop of come. When I finally released my oral grip on Buck's cock, he lifted me to my feet.

"That's a good start," he said as he peeled his T-shirt off me and untied the drawstring of the sweatpants I was wearing. They dropped to the floor and pooled around my ankles, revealing my own still-erect cock.

I stepped out of the sweatpants and turned. I'd seen lube in Buck's medicine cabinet when I'd been rooting around for the antiseptic, and I knew we'd need it. I pulled open the cabinet and wrapped my fingers around the tube of lube just as Buck spun me back around to face him.

He lifted me onto the countertop, spread my legs, and stepped between them. His cock was already half-erect and was rising rapidly as he slid a condom over it. I opened the lube, squirted a glob on my fingers, and slathered it over his swollen cock head. He grabbed my legs behind the knees and lifted until he had my body at the angle he wanted. Then he pressed his lube-covered cock against the tight pucker of my ass and drove forward, causing me to gasp as he buried himself inside me.

I was surprised and excited at the same time. No lover had ever taken me like this, and I had never been able to stare into my lover's eyes as we fucked. Buck pulled back and pushed forward, his slick shaft rubbing against the underside of my ball sac as he drove into me, exciting me. I reached between us, wrapped my fist around my own turgid cock, and began pumping.

Buck stared into my eyes, never once looking away, his pale blue eyes mesmerizing me. I came first, firing warm spunk all over my abdomen. That seemed to excite Buck because he began pumping harder, faster.

Then, with one final, powerful thrust that made my ass squeak against the countertop as he pushed me backward, Buck came. Neither of us moved as the cowboy's cock throbbed within me, and we stared deep into one another's eyes until his cock finally softened enough for him to easily pull free.

I'd been ridden hard; would I be put away wet?

Not by this cowboy.

We cleaned up, and then Buck led me to the hacienda bed, where I finally told him exactly why I'd been on my way to a housewarming in New Mexico.

"You still in love with your ex-roommate?"

"No," I admitted. "I think I just wanted to cause him as much pain as he'd caused me when he moved out."

"And now?"

"Now I realize what a stupid idea that was."

"But it brought you here, to my bed," Buck said.

I smiled, snuggled against him, and fell asleep with Buck's arms wrapped around me.

The sun blasted through the eastern-facing French doors the next morning, waking me. Buck had one arm over his eyes and the bright light didn't seem to bother him. I slipped out of bed, opened the French doors, and stood naked on the balcony. I couldn't see any of the longhorn cattle from where I stood, but I could make out a couple of the oil wells in the far, far distance of my host's big spread.

I glanced back into the bedroom. Buck had kicked off the sheet and his thick phallus lay flaccid against his thigh, reminding me of the hard ride he'd given me the previous evening.

Buck's mechanic would be retrieving my dead hybrid later that morning and could take all the time in the world repairing it because I was in no hurry to leave. I crawled back into bed with Buck, took the head of his cock in my mouth, and slowly woke my handsome cowboy.

What Springs Up

Every spring the community garden in my neighborhood brings together green thumbs and brown thumbs, all intent on growing our own produce within blocks of our townhouses. I enjoy the fresh air and the opportunity to interact with my neighbors, but what I enjoy most is watching Nicolas Carter.

He's broad-shouldered and thick chested, with a trim waist and six-pack abs that he's earned through several years of spring gardening and winter workouts at the gym. He wears his sandy hair in a short brush cut and his pale blue eyes are always sparkling with amusement. When he's in the garden, he wears cargo shorts and work boots, and more often than not his T-shirt is slung over the fence or laying in a heap on the ground at the end of his plot. His chest and back are quite smooth, and I suspect that's more a matter of personal grooming than genetics. Often the first in the community garden on Saturdays and Sundays, he's always available to assist the other gardeners.

I'm not much of a gardener and my little plot, despite my best efforts, is often among the least productive. I usually tend my plot Saturday mornings, but one Saturday this past May I was called into the office and didn't reach the community garden until late in the evening. The sun was already setting by the time I retrieved my gloves and handtools from the shed where we all kept our gardening supplies in assigned cubbyholes, but soon I was on my knees in the dirt.

I thought I was alone in the garden and had weeded half of one row of scraggly tomato plants when a pair of boots appeared in front of me. Startled, I looked up to see Nicolas standing before me, wearing only his boots and cargo shorts, his T-shirt hanging half-out of one pocket. I straightened up but remained on my knees, my face mere inches from the bulge at the crotch of the taller man.

"You look like you could use some help," he said.

The bulge in his shorts seemed to be enlarging, and I wet my lips before answering. "Do you have the right tool?"

He smiled. "There's only one way to find out."

We were obviously thinking the same thing. I removed my gloves and reached for his zipper.

"Not out here," Nicolas said. He took my hand and helped me to my feet. "The tool shed."

He led me into the shed and closed the door behind us, leaving us in near darkness. The only light filtered in through the gap around the door, but it was enough for what we were about to do.

"I've been watching you all spring," Nicolas said, "and I know you've been watching me."

He pulled me into his muscular arms and covered my mouth with his. He smelled earthy and musky, and his kiss was deep and penetrating. I felt his cock growing against me through our clothing.

When our kiss ended, I dropped to my knees on the shed's dirt floor, unfastened his cargo shorts and let them drop to his ankles. Nicolas had gone commando under the shorts and his tumescent cock slapped my cheek. I wrapped one hand around the thick stem to hold it steady and took the swollen purple blossom into my mouth. I watered it with saliva and then slowly took every inch of his stem into my oral cavity until his soft crotch hair tickled my nose.

When I felt Nicolas begin to tense, I grabbed his ass cheeks and pulled his crotch tight to my face. His cock head pressed against the back of my throat, and he came. He came hard, and I swallowed every drop of his thick, hot come. Nicolas wasn't done with me, though. When his cock stopped spasming in my mouth, he pulled me to my feet and spun me around. After I unfastened my pants, dropped them to the dirt floor, and stepped out of them, he bent me over a wheelbarrow, grabbed a bottle of hand lotion one of the older women kept in her cubbyhole next to her sunbonnet, and squirted it on his hands. Then he ran his slick fingers up and down the furrow of my ass crack, repeatedly teasing my bunghole. Finally, he slipped a finger in, and then a second, preparing me for the garden tool to come.

He slathered more lotion on his rejuvenated cock and pressed his cock head against my ass pucker. When I pressed back against him, letting him know I was ready, he planted his cock deep inside me. Then he held onto my hips and plowed into my ass hard and fast and deep. Before long the wheelbarrow rolled out from beneath me. I thought I would fall, but Nicolas wouldn't let that happen. He just gripped me tighter and continued plowing into me.

My cock had grown hard and needed attention. I wrapped my fist around my own cock stem and stroked hard and fast, never quite in rhythm to the gardener behind me.

Nicolas came first, plowing into my ass one last time. He held me tight against him as he fired a thick stream of hot come into me.

And then I came, spewing come over the wheelbarrow that was now just out of arm's reach.

We stood together in the darkness of the toolshed until Nicolas's cock finally stopped spasming. Then he pulled away and I turned to face him.

When we caught our breath, Nicolas said, "You ready to get to those weeds?"

We dressed, finished weeding my little plot, and then went our separate ways. I didn't see him again all that week.

When I arrived at the community garden the following Saturday morning, half-a-dozen people had already surrounded Nicolas, asking his advice on compost and fertilizer and other gardening topics.

He nodded to me as I walked past, and when I returned from the shed with my gloves and my hand tools, he interrupted his conversation and asked if I needed any help.

"Maybe later," I told him with a wink. "I have something in my garden that keeps coming up."

Relationships

My neighborhood had once been home to several warehouses and manufacturing companies but had been gentrified. Among the first businesses to convert a warehouse into something else was a bathhouse, identifiable to those in the know only because the address was 69 Long Avenue, located at one end of a stub of a street that only stretched for a few blocks, and which had at the other end a new Starbucks and two art galleries. I'm certain the owners of 69 were aware of the implications of the address well before they purchased and converted the building.

I lived in a loft apartment three stories above the Starbucks, within easy walking distance of the bathhouse in one direction and public transportation in the other. On Long Avenue, and within a several-block area surrounding the street, were bistros, galleries, antique stores, funky little clothing shops, and my bookstore, a specialty shop not yet in danger from electronic publishing because I specialized in finding out-of-print mystery, science fiction, and sleazecore novels for collectors willing to pay my prices.

Much like many of the neighborhood's other business owners, my interest in the area had been piqued by my 69 membership, and for several years before I joined the neighborhood, I had watched it transform from a collection of abandoned buildings housing an equal number of rats and pigeons to a place where people lived and worked.

Because 69 had been the catalyst that began the transformation, over the years the neighborhood had attracted a certain type of resident, and each day I found myself interacting with a veritable cornucopia of people representing every gender and sexual orientation imaginable in a live-and-let-live environment I'd not experienced elsewhere. It should have been the perfect environment to find the love of my life, but, alas, it was not. A bookworm at heart, I was a failure at relationships. They never lasted long and often ended bitterly when my beau-of-the-month realized I was far more interested in life between the covers of a book than in anything he had to say.

Yet I retained my sexual urges. I still desired the feel of a young man's naked body pressed against mine in carnal congress, so I maintained membership at 69 and visited whenever desire overwhelmed me. Though I might occasionally recognize some of the other members while parading around in nothing but a towel and flip-flops, we often acted as strangers within the confines of 69's sultry, two-story establishment and, more often than not, the usually closeted and sometimes bisexual men I hooked up with came from out of town or from the suburbs.

I had spent the day tracking down copies of two Orrie Hitt sleazecore novels and a trio of Vin Packer's lesbian novels, work I had thrown myself into the day after being dumped by yet another potential paramour, and I had been left sexually unsatisfied by the loss. After treating myself to a light dinner and a glass of wine at a bistro around the corner from my bookstore, I decided a trip to 69—though not a person, my relationship to it was the longest I'd had with anyone or anything—was in order.

Open twenty-four hours a day, seven days a week, 69 is accessible through an electronically dead-bolted solid steel door—a remnant of the days when patron safety was of paramount concern—with the bathhouse's two-digit address typographically enhanced to cover the entire door. I leaned into the bell, waited while the camera above the door caught my image, and then entered after being buzzed in.

I approached the lobby desk and presented my identification to an impeccably dressed young man I found particularly appealing but dared not proposition because bathhouse policy forbade guests and staff from carnal interaction. After he confirmed my membership and I paid for an eight-hour room rental, the young man buzzed me through to the bathhouse proper where an unfamiliar man with the battered face and cauliflower ear of someone who had once worked as a punching bag in a boxing gym handed me a white towel, a pair of blue flip-flops, and my room key suspended from an elastic band.

The two floors of 69 are a dimly lit maze with no direct path from here to there anywhere in the building, with several steam baths, Jacuzzi tubs, dry saunas, and a swimming pool. Various rooms had been designed and decorated to represent places where once unsafe assignations could be accommodated safely, from truck-stop glory holes to airport restrooms where would-be senators could slide their feet under the stalls, to a jail cell with padded bars where willing participants could act out prison fantasies, to the balcony seating of a pornographic movie house where explicit movies played nonstop. Light snacks and nonalcoholic drinks were available for purchase as were a variety of sex toys and toiletries, none of which I needed that evening.

Lockers were grouped near the front of the first floor, but private rooms were located on the second floor, and I made my way upstairs past life-size posters of handsome, naked men to the room I had rented. I used my key and pushed open the door, finding a simply decorated room painted a soothing pale blue, with a locker that opened with the same key as the door, a single bed consisting of a vinyl mattress on a wooden frame, and a nightstand next to the bed with a trio of condoms and a small, unopened tube of lube in a wicker basket atop it.

I stripped off my clothes and secured them in the locker. Then I wrapped the towel around my waist, slipped the room key's elastic band around my wrist, and hooked a small pill container to the elastic band. After adjusting my glasses, I headed to the sauna.

Except in private areas, 69 discouraged complete nudity, and with everyone wearing the same towel and little else for demarcation of status, we became equals in every way except physical attributes, and men who might not approach one another in the outside world had no qualms about doing so within the confines of the bathhouse.

And so, on my way to the sauna downstairs, other men touched me, some tentatively and others aggressively. Not yet in the mood for companionship, I shook my head at the tentative gropers and pushed away the hands of the aggressive gropers. Once inside the sauna room, where a dozen men had already gathered, I found an open space on the bench, unwrapped my towel so that I was sitting on it nude, and relaxed. Though I let my gaze wander, comparing and contrasting the other men—from the doughy, overweight man in the corner to the muscular hunk of man meat at the end of the bench, their cocks equally diverse in size and shape and their personal grooming habits, or lack of them, on display—the sauna was not a place to hook up, and we all sat in silence, absorbed in our own thoughts. I felt good about my appearance, especially for my age, with only a touch of gray showing at my temples and elsewhere, and the few extra pounds clinging to my waist easily disappeared when I dressed.

Every few minutes the population of the sauna changed, with men exiting and others entering in no discernable pattern. By the time I felt completely relaxed, no one in the sauna had been there when I arrived. I again wrapped the towel around my waist, exited the sauna and stepped down the hall to the shower, a replica of the showers in a high school gym locker where men felt free to approach one another. I had the showers to myself, so I took a quick, ice-cold rinse, exchanged my now-wet towel for a clean one, and returned the way I had come.

It's disconcerting to have reached an age where Viagra is my only sure path to an erection, but at least I still have my hair, and I look good wearing the gold-frame bifocals prescribed to me only a few years earlier to combat increasing nearsightedness. I purchased a bottle of water at the concession stand, downed a Viagra from the pill container I'd attached to my wristband, and walked upstairs to my rented room. Leaving the door open, I shed the towel and lay face-up on the single bed, indicating that I was interested in fellatio. There I waited, wondering which I would have first, company or an erection.

One might call it a tie. My cock was partially erect when an attractive blond in his early thirties filled the open doorway and examined me for a moment.

"I saw you in the sauna," he said, "and I liked what I saw. Mind if I join you?"

After I told him I didn't mind, he crossed the room and sat on the side of the bed, next to me. He placed one hand on my leg, his fingers tickling the inside of my thigh. Between his touch and the Viagra coursing through my veins, my cock finished rising to its full stature, seeming all that much bigger because I kept my pubic region closely trimmed.

The blond slid his hand along my leg until he cupped my heavy ball sac, but he did not touch my cock. He kneaded my balls as if weighing and judging them, and he stroked my perineum with the tip of his middle finger. I hadn't noticed it when he'd entered my room, but he'd brought his own lube with him, and he stopped massaging my balls just long enough to squeeze a dollop into his palms. He coated my cock shaft with the lube and then returned to massaging my balls and stroking my perineum.

He bent forward and took the head of my cock in his mouth, licked away the drop of pre-come that had oozed out of the tip while he'd coated my cock with lube, and then lowered his face until he had easily taken my entire length into his oral cavity. The blond pulled his face upward until just my cock head remained between his lips, and then he did it again.

I had just closed my eyes, enjoying the warm, wet sensation of the young blond's mouth on my cock, when a sound from the doorway caught my attention.

I opened my eyes to see a dark-haired man standing in the open doorway watching, his towel tented. He appeared to be older than the blond giving me fellatio but was still a good bit younger than me.

"Mind if I watch?" he asked.

When I shook my head, he unfastened the towel, slung it around his shoulders, and took his erect cock in his fist. As the blond continued fellating me, the dark-haired man in the doorway jerked off.

The blond's head rose and fell, rose and fell, and he continued massaging my balls. As lube slid from my balls onto my perineum and down my ass crack to soak the sheet beneath me, the blond's head moved faster and faster. Soon I was thrusting my hips upward, my groin meeting each of his face's descents.

The dark-haired man in the doorway came with a grunt, shooting a thin stream of come halfway across the room, and I knew I was also about to come when my ball sac tightened and my cock stiffened. The blond must have sensed it, too, because he pressed one lube slickened finger against the tight pucker of my ass hole and slid it deep inside me, pressing my prostate from the inside.

I couldn't stop myself. I closed my eyes, thrust upward one last time, and came, firing wad after thick wad of warm come against the back of the blond's throat. He eagerly swallowed every drop, not letting the tiniest bit escape from between his lips.

By the time my cock stopped throbbing in the blond's mouth and I finally opened my eyes, the dark-haired man had abandoned the doorway. When the blond was certain I had finished, he removed his finger from my ass and released his oral grip on my rapidly deflating cock.

He sat upright and stared down into my eyes.

I said, "I haven't seen you here before."

"This is my first time," he said. "I just moved into the neighborhood."

"If I see you here again—" I didn't finish my sentence.

"Of course."

He patted my thigh, then stood and adjusted his towel. On his way out, he closed the door so that I would not be disturbed during post-orgasm recovery.

I lay in the bed for half an hour before I finally rose. Then I used my towel to wipe the lube from my cock, crotch, and ass crack before I opened the locker and retrieved my clothes.

After I dressed, I pocketed the unused condoms and lube, and left 69 with time remaining on my eight-hour room rental, satiated and thankfully without any obligation for post-coital relationship-status conversation. I returned to my loft apartment, tucked into bed alone, and promised myself I would not attempt another relationship when satisfactory anonymous sex was available twenty-four-hours a day a mere three blocks from home.

It was a lie I only believed until I met the new blond Starbucks barista the next morning on my way to my bookstore. The milk foam head he put on my Grande latte was just as impressive as the head he'd given me the night before. The blond winked as he handed me the latte.

I thought maybe I should try one more time for a lasting relationship. I asked, "Do you like old books?"

The XXXmas Gift

For three consecutive years my roommate hung an extra-large jockstrap from the mantle on Christmas Eve. "Everyone else hangs stockings," Kevin said each time he did it, "but someday Santa's going to fill this for me."

The fourth year I decided to do something about it.

Kevin had been flirting with Delray, one of the weekend bartenders at The Glory Hole, and I was certain the attraction was mutual based on comments I'd heard Delray make when Kevin was out of earshot. When I heard Delray wouldn't be making his annual trip home for the holidays, I approached him with my idea.

Arranging things was more difficult than I anticipated—especially getting Delray into the house in the wee hours of Christmas morning without waking Kevin—but it was worth the effort, and I cherish my photo of the surprised look on Kevin's face when he stumbled into the living room that morning and found Delray posed next to the fireplace wearing nothing but a Santa hat and the jockstrap Kevin had hung from the mantle the night before.

I couldn't help myself, but the view of Delray's near-naked body had the candy cane in my pocket pointing due north. Delray spent his time away from the bar pumping iron and it showed in his broad shoulders, thick arms, six-pack abs, tight ass, and tree-stump thighs. He'd exfoliated the previous day and the twinkling Christmas tree lights reflected off his glistening, lightly oiled bronze skin.

And I wasn't the only one who appreciated the view. Kevin slept in the nude and, because he hadn't tied the sash of his robe tight enough when he'd come out of his room, his red-nosed reindeer was peeking through the gap.

"Don't just stand there with your mouth open," I told my roommate. "Unwrap your gift."

Kevin crossed the room and stopped in front of Delray. He placed one hand on the bartender's thick chest and then let it trail down Delray's abdomen and under the wide elastic waistband of the jockstrap. His eyes widened in surprise when he discovered the long, thick phallus constrained by the pouch.

"I must have been a very good boy," he said huskily.

"I've been waiting all year for this," Delray said. He grabbed Kevin's head between his two big hands and planted his lips on Kevin's. My roommate practically melted against his Christmas gift as the kiss grew longer and deeper. When the kiss ended, Kevin dropped to his knees, drawing the jockstrap down to reveal Delray's turgid erection. He cupped Delray's balls as if judging their weight as he drew the bartender's cock head between his lips.

By then I had settled onto the couch to watch, and as the only one of us fully dressed, I felt the need to loosen my belt and unzip my fly to release the pressure on my own cock.

Kevin took the first inch of Delray's cock into his mouth and then drew back. He took a little more in the next time and a little more the time after that as his head bobbed forward and back.

Apparently, he was moving too slow for Delray. The bartender grabbed the back of Kevin's head and thrust his cock deep into Kevin's mouth. After Kevin accepted it all, Delray drew back until only his swollen cock head remained between my roommate's lips. Then he thrust forward again.

He thrust harder and faster, face-fucking my roommate, his heavy balls bouncing off Kevin's chin with each thrust.

I couldn't help myself. I reached into my pants and wrapped my fist around my cock shaft. As I watched the two men going at it in front of the fireplace, illuminated by the glowing embers and the twinkling of Christmas tree lights, I stroked up and down, matching my pace to Delray's, going harder and faster as Delray pumped harder and faster.

Delray came before I did, holding Kevin's head still as he unloaded against the back of Kevin's throat. My roommate couldn't swallow fast enough. Delray's come seeped from the corner of Kevin's mouth and dripped to the hardwood floor.

I came then, firing a thick wad of warm spunk all over my fist and the inside of my boxers. As Delray withdrew his still spasming cock from Kevin's mouth, I excused myself and slipped into the bathroom to clean up.

By the time I returned to the living room, Delray had lost the Santa hat and Kevin had shed his robe. The big man had my roommate bent over the back of the couch and was slamming his thick cock into Kevin's ass.

I hadn't bothered to replace my clothes after cleaning myself up and I was just as naked as the other two men. I stepped up behind Delray and slipped one hand between his thighs and between Kevin's. I wrapped my fist around my roommate's swollen cock and jacked him off as Delray continued to pump into his ass.

Kevin came first, spewing come over the back of the couch. Then Delray came with one last powerful thrust, unloading himself into Kevin.

When Delray's cock finally slipped from my roommate's ass and he turned to face me, he saw that my cock was once again hard. He grabbed my cock and said, "I didn't realize you came as part of a package deal."

"That wasn't the original plan," I told him. "But now that we're all in the Christmas spirit—"

His mouth covered mine and I never finished my sentence.

I'm not certain how many more times and in how many more combinations the three of us fucked that Christmas morning, but I know Kevin and I were exhausted by the time Delray left.

I made hot chocolate for the two of us and served it with a peppermint stick in each cup. Wearing only our robes, Kevin and I relaxed on the couch, sipping our drinks and staring at the unwrapped gifts still piled under the tree.

My roommate finally broke the silence.

"Next year," Kevin said, "I'll put up two jockstraps so I don't have to share my Christmas gift."

Friends and Lovers

Eddie and I were best friends throughout high school, thrown together in detention during our first week as ninth graders for a pair of heinous offenses against the school system that I no longer remember, and rarely separated from that point onward. I was the skinny new kid, having arrived in the small northern California town with my parents only three weeks before the school year started; Eddie was a town lifer, the pudgy only child of a waitress and a laborer at the lumber mill.

We did everything together—shot pool down in fish town when we should have been at Wednesday night Bible study, drank stolen bottles of Schlitz and smoked pilfered Virginia Slims under the bridge as often as we could, and wore the ink off the pages of three pornographic magazines we found stashed in his grandfather's garage. I didn't tell him then because I didn't think he would understand—I'm not certain I understood myself—but I was more interested in the men in those photographs than the women.

I lost track of Eddie the summer after graduation. He enlisted in the Army, intending to make a career of it to avoid spending his life in the lumber mill or on the fishing boats, and went off to boot camp while I moved halfway across the country to attend a university in Austin that seemed to employ more people than even lived in the town I left behind. I found a home in the English department—a place where skinny guys like me didn't stand out—and lost my cherry to a graduate assistant after a long evening spent discussing *Beowulf* and smoking fat little spliffs in his one-bedroom walk-up.

After graduation I joined the university's public relations department, traded my student hovel for a small loft apartment and, a few years later, traded up again for a two-bedroom fixer-upper not far from campus. I drifted in and out of relationships for the next two decades, with none lasting more than a few months.

The lumber company transferred my father midway through my second semester, and I lost my only incentive for returning to the northern California town where I'd attended high school. Because I made no effort to maintain contact with my former classmates, I was surprised when I opened my mailbox one evening in the spring of 2000 and discovered an invitation to my graduating class's twenty-five-year reunion. By then my fixer-upper had been fixed up, my neighborhood had become trendy, and my house was the envy of neighborhood latecomers.

I removed my jacket, loosened my tie, and settled onto one of the two director's chairs I kept on my porch. I read and reread the invitation, examined the schedule of events, and pondered the wisdom of using vacation time to return to a place that held few particularly good memories. There was only one reason to take the time and spend the money: I wanted to know what had happened to Eddie, and I had no way to know if he would be there or not.

* * *

Three weeks later, after spring became summer, I flew into San Francisco, rented a car, and drove north along the coastline until Highway 1 became Main Street. The town hadn't changed much. A McDonald's had joined the locally owned cafes and restaurants, the lumber mill where my father had once been a senior manager had closed, and Main Street had two more stoplights.

I had reserved a room at a motel north of town, across the creek from the bowling alley where Eddie and I first encountered Pong. My second-floor room overlooked the Pacific Ocean, held a king-size bed, and had the same decor as every other low-budget chain motel room across small-town America. I probably could have stayed in a newer hotel, but I had booked my room in the only place I could remember by name.

After I unpacked, I napped for an hour, then showered and dressed for the evening, an adults-only affair in the banquet room of a restaurant that hadn't existed twenty-five years earlier, and the first of a weekend's worth of activities that included a family-friendly picnic the following day in the state park three miles north of town.

At the registration table I realized that some overly ambitious former classmate—probably a bored housewife for whom the reunion was the highlight of her social calendar for the decade—had included our yearbook photos on the name badges. I grimaced when I saw the longhaired, pimple-faced young man I had once been, then silently thanked fate when I realized the elephantine mouth-breather on the far side of the registration table had been the head cheerleader, a buxom blonde who had more balls between her thighs our senior year than the football team's center.

After pinning the name badge to my jacket, I stopped at the cash bar for a glass of Pinot Grigio. Then I circumnavigated the banquet room, stopping now and then to stare at name badges and speak briefly with people I barely remembered and who barely remembered me.

Then I saw Eddie.

He was speaking with two pot-bellied ex-jocks, not looking in my direction. His shoulder-length black hair had been buzzed into a flattop liberally sprinkled with salt, and the doughy young man I had known then had become a thick, muscular adult. I had changed as well, adding weight and muscle tone thanks to the exercise room and lap pool in the university's student center, and I regularly visited a stylist who not only trimmed my hair but also maintained the highlights that masked the encroaching gray. I didn't approach Eddie immediately, instead waiting until he finished his conversation and the two jocks moved on.

He turned, saw me approaching and smiled. Without glancing at my name badge or even hearing my voice, he said, "I didn't think you'd come."

Eddie gathered me into his arms, gave me a bear hug that spilled my wine and threatened to crack a few ribs, and then held me at arm's length and looked me up and down. "Time's been good to you."

"You, too," I said, and it was true.

When Eddie saw that my Pinot Grigio had spilled, he took my elbow, led me to the bar, and asked what I'd been drinking. Then he ordered a replacement for me and for himself a Jack and Coke.

After we had our drinks, Eddie raised his in a toast and said, "To misspent youth."

I touched my wine glass to his tumbler, and we both drank.

We spent the rest of the evening reminiscing, oblivious to our former classmates milling about, and we remained long after they returned home or headed to their motel rooms. When restaurant staff closed the banquet room, we moved to the bar.

We talked about cruising Main Street with Bachman-Turner Overdrive blaring from the 8-track player, about hours spent playing pinball at the miniature golf course south of town, and about more hours spent immersed in digest-sized science fiction magazines we bought at the liquor store. We talked about our parents—mine retired and living in Seattle, his still working and living in the same house where he'd been raised.

I told him about life in Austin, a liberal pimple on the conservative ass of Texas, and he told me about his military career and his role in Desert Storm after Iraq invaded Kuwait. There was a delicious irony in that, after a childhood spent as a corporate vagabond, I had opted to settle in one place for the entirety of my adult life and Eddie, having spent his entire childhood in one place, had seen the world through military service and had continued traveling after retirement, purchasing a small motor home and towing a Jeep behind it as he cruised the back roads of America.

Despite all the places he had traveled and all the things he had experienced, Eddie was the same person I had known all those years ago, the same person I had called my best friend, and our conversation flowed as if mere hours had passed since we'd last been together. We were so entranced with one another that we remained long past last call and the bartender finally had to escort us out the door before barricading it behind us. We walked around the restaurant to the dark back lot where ours were the only two cars remaining, his a WWII-era Jeep with a tow bar sticking up in front of the grill, mine a rental with no discernable personality.

I probably should have shaken Eddie's hand, maybe given him a hug, but I'd had a bit too much Pinot Grigio and I wasn't thinking. Eddie had been my best friend for four years, someone I had cared about more than any other person in my life other than my parents, and someone who, I was reluctant to admit, I actually loved. So, I grabbed his face with both hands and planted a kiss on his lips.

Eddie didn't resist, but he didn't return the kiss, either.

Realizing what I had done, I stepped back, horrified at what he must have thought, and then turned and hurried to my car. I drove away without looking back, and I spent the rest of the night chastising myself.

* * *

I arrived at the reunion picnic just before noon the next day, arriving late because I was unsure how to deal with the conflicting emotions seeing Eddie had stirred up, and finally decided to confront them head on. I found Eddie sitting alone at one of the picnic tables gnawing on a ham sandwich and nursing a beer.

"About last night—" I started.

"Don't worry about it," he said around a mouthful of sandwich.

"But—"

He held up his hand, palm toward me, a silent command to stop talking. After he swallowed, Eddie said, "I knew. Even back then, I knew. You don't have to apologize."

"You did?"

"I didn't know the words for it, but I knew." He held up his beer bottle and used it as a pointer. "There's more where this came from in that cooler over there."

After I grabbed a beer, I was stopped by one of the reunion organizers, a woman I had barely known when we were high school students. I then visited with more of my former classmates, met their spouses and children and grandchildren, and deflected questions about my own marital status and prospects for parenthood by saying I was happy with my career and hadn't yet met the right person. Many of my former classmates were happy to tell me about their lives and the insignificant things they'd accomplished in the years since graduation. Few of them seemed to notice that I shared little in return.

Someone had brought lawn darts, and I found myself taking third place in an impromptu lawn darts tournament. Someone else had set up a volleyball net on the beach, but the only people playing were the children and grandchildren of my former classmates. The afternoon disappeared in a flurry of activity that included gathering the Class of '75 in one place for a group picture while the sunlight was still favorable.

After posing for the group picture, standing in the back row with Eddie's arm around my shoulder, I bade my farewells and told Eddie I would be leaving town first thing the next morning.

"Where are you staying?" he asked.

I told him.

"Mind if I stop on the way back into town?"

I had no idea why he would want to, but I told him he could.

* * *

I had been in my room for nearly an hour when Eddie rapped on the door. I opened it and found him standing outside with a cold six-pack of beer, a bucket of warm potato salad, a paper plate filled with lunchmeat, and half a loaf of bread that he had liberated from the reunion committee.

"Dinner's ready," he said with a smile as he pushed past me into my room.

He piled everything on the room's only table. As we ate, we continued the conversation the bartender had interrupted the night before as if nothing had happened after being escorted from the bar. When he finished his second beer, Eddie kicked off his shoes and stretched out on the bed.

Before long, I stretched out beside him, and our conversation drifted from past to present and covered all the intervening years. After another hour, Eddie finally revealed himself to me, telling me how difficult it had been to remain in the service after he finally admitted to himself that he was in the closet.

"I think about you all the time," Eddie said. "Dream about you, fantasize about you, wonder what might have been if I hadn't taken so long to—if I had just admitted to myself—if—"

"I've wondered the same things," I admitted.

"You surprised me last night in the parking lot," he said. "I should have told you right then how I felt."

"Tell me now."

When Eddie rose up on one elbow and looked down at me, I knew what was going to happen and I wasn't about to resist. He kissed me, gently at first, his lips just brushing against mine. He kissed me again and again, on my lips, my cheek, my earlobe, my shoulder, the hollow at the base of my throat. When his lips returned to mine, his kiss became more urgent and soon our tongues met in a fiery dance of desire. At the same time, our fingers fumbled with buttons, buckles, snaps, and zippers. Our clothes hit the floor at a steady pace.

And when we were both naked, we paused and looked at one another. We had seen each other unclothed many times—in the locker room showers after gym class, skinny dipping in the river, while preparing for bed during sleepovers at his house or mine—but we were no longer undeveloped and inexperienced young men. We were adults, with men's bodies and more experience than either of us was ever likely to admit.

Black hair covered his barrel chest and abdomen, and his crotch was a wild and untamed forest from which the thick tube of his cock rose majestically. I ran my thin fingers through his chest hair, teased his nipples with my thumbs, and then let my hands stray lower until I wrapped one fist around his cock. I slowly stroked the entire length, from the hard pubic bone at the base to the spongy soft mushroom cap of the glans.

Unlike Eddie, I don't have much body hair, and I keep my nether region neatly groomed. Though neither as long nor as thick as his cock, mine didn't have to compete with surrounding shrubbery for attention, and one of Eddie's strong hands enveloped it. I was too excited, and it only took a few powerful strokes of his fist before I came.

My cock spasmed in his fist and a thin stream of warm come covered my abdomen. Eddie released his grip on my cock and let it flounder against my abdomen. I started to apologize, but he stopped me with a smile and said, "You always did like to be first, didn't you?"

Eddie slipped off the bed, dug a lubricated condom packet from his pants pocket, and then rejoined me. Ever since that night with the graduate assistant when I realized what I was and why I had felt the way I had about Eddie, I had dreamed of this moment.

He didn't disappoint me. He tore open the condom packet and unrolled the condom over his thick cock. Then he knelt between my widespread thighs, lifted my legs and bent me nearly in half. He pressed the tip of his condom-covered cock against the tight pucker of my ass hole and then pushed forward. The lubrication allowed him to enter me easily and smoothly, and he buried the entire length of his cock inside me. Then, resting much of his weight on my thighs, he drew back and pushed forward as he stared down into my eyes. Previous lovers had all taken me from behind, and being able to watch Eddie's face as we made love filled me with unexpected pleasure. I reached up and cupped his face in my hands, stroking his cheeks with the balls of my thumbs as I held him.

As he pumped into me, my cock regained its former stature and his hairy abdomen rubbed against the head with each of his powerful thrusts. Eddie began pumping faster, driving deeper into me with each thrust, and I felt myself approaching a second orgasm. I moved my hands from his face and gripped the cheeks of his ass just as we came.

His face contorted as he came, and he stiffened above me just before filling the condom with his come. And then I came, too, covering my belly with a second load of spunk.

For several heartbeats neither of us could move. Finally, Eddie withdrew, slipped from the bed into the bathroom and discarded the condom.

When he returned, he lay behind me, and we spooned until I fell asleep in his arms.

* * *

When the alarm woke me Sunday morning, the other side of the bed was empty. Eddie had cleaned up the mess we'd made of the picnic food, and all that remained of him was the lingering scent of his aftershave and our coupling. He hadn't left a note, hadn't told me how I could reach him, and hadn't even asked how to find me in Austin.

I checked out of the motel that morning, returned to San Francisco, the airport, and home. I never expected to see Eddie again. Maybe it was better that way. Maybe one powerful memory of the night when I realized Eddie felt the same way about me that I felt about him would be enough to sustain me for years to come. Maybe we finally had the answers to all the unanswered questions we had been carrying with us for twenty-five years.

For the next several weeks, I compared every man I met to Eddie—Eddie as a young man, Eddie as an adult—and none of them measured up nor were they invited into my bed.

* * *

Nearly two months after the reunion I returned home from the university to find a motor home with California license plates and a Jeep in tow parked in front of my house. I pulled into my drive, walked to the porch, and found Eddie sitting on one of the director's chairs drinking from a sweating can of beer. He reached into the cooler at his feet and pulled out another can. After he handed it to me, I settled onto the other director's chair. As I popped the top of the beer, Eddie said, "Nice place."

"I think so."

"It's a little frou-frou, though," he said. "Could use a man's touch."

"Yours?"

Eddie nodded.

He's been here ever since.

Riding Out the Storm

We sat in Pat O'Brien's, ordered Hurricanes—enjoying the delicious irony of it all—and laughed at the possibility that anyone would take a hurricane warning seriously. The storm would turn, missing the city like always, and the Big Easy would remain open for business.

"But what if it doesn't?" Bordeaux asked. Bordeaux performed five nights a week in a drag show at a little place around the corner from Bourbon Street, the only queen in town to portray Whitney Houston at her coked-out worst. Even though he'd pulled off the wig and had changed into street clothes, Bordeaux still wore his makeup. The city's few remaining tourists and conventioneers tried not to look at him as they squeezed past. Bourbon Street regulars didn't even notice. "The governor's already declared a state of emergency."

Sammy and I stared at Bordeaux as if he'd lost his mind, then we ordered another round of drinks. Bordeaux didn't finish his, leaving Sammy and me alone at the corner table to discuss other storms that had threatened New Orleans. After round three I took Sammy back to his apartment on Toulouse and fucked him to the sounds of a jazz band playing in a bar somewhere down the street.

Bordeaux left town the next morning, packing his elderly grandparents into a Ford LTD with bad shocks. Sammy and I stood in front of his house in the Lower Ninth Ward and waved goodbye. Then we loaded the perishables that Bordeaux had insisted we take into Sammy's Saturn and sped over to Sammy's apartment to get them into the refrigerator. We visited two different grocery stores that afternoon and stocked up on nonperishable food, buying things we could eat directly from the box or the can in case we lost power. Sammy already had quite a collection of candles, so we bought oil for the hurricane lamp and two large boxes of wooden matches. At the last minute, Sammy made me stop at a liquor store and we picked up three boxes of cheap red wine. Bad wine always tastes better during a storm.

That evening, as we ate beignets and drank coffee with chicory at Café Du Monde, I held Sammy's hand and realized we made quite a couple. He was a good eleven years older than me, whippet thin with graying hair cut finger length and blown dry. His angular features softened only when he looked at me, and he looked at me often.

I worked as a bouncer at the Hustler Club, a place where I was surrounded by naked female flesh and had no desire to touch any of it, which made me perfect for the job. I had the build for a bouncer too—broad shoulders, thick chest, arms as big around as some men's thighs. I'd played defensive end through high school and junior college and still spent two hours a day in the gym maintaining my physique. The dancers loved me. The patrons who got too touchy-feely with them did not.

My fingers were covered with powdered sugar from the beignets, and Sammy lifted my hand to his mouth to lick my fingers clean. An erotic tingle crawled up my arm and down to my groin, and I felt my cock start to react.

I pulled my hand away and whispered, "Not here, Sammy."

Disappointment colored his face.

I wiped my hand on a napkin, finished my chicory coffee, and then we walked back to his place. Sammy had a second-floor apartment in a U-shaped building that wrapped around a central courtyard paved in uneven brick and filled with lush, tropical plants. All six apartments—three downstairs and three upstairs—faced the courtyard. That night we sat among the plants, talking with the other tenants. We opened one of the boxes of red wine, and the only straight man in the six-unit complex iced up a case of Dixie beer. At some point during the evening, we spoke to every one of our neighbors, though they didn't all visit the courtyard at the same time. Some of them were too busy packing and loading their cars to do more than grab a beer or ask for help carrying some box or treasured item. They all had different ideas about what would happen when the storm hit, but none predicted what actually happened afterward.

Sammy and I were the last to disappear into our apartment that night, and we were both suitably lit from all the wine and beer. When I sat on the edge of Sammy's bed to pull off my shoes, he slipped onto the bed behind me and wrapped his arms around my neck. He whispered into my ear, his warm breath sending sexual shivers through my entire body.

"You're going to take care of me, aren't you?" he whispered.

"I always do, don't I?"

I'd been taking care of Sammy ever since the night I caught two inebriated Cajuns trying to pound him into the cobblestones because they didn't like his type. I'd sent them back to the bayou looking like they'd lost ten rounds with a pissed-off gator while I'd spent the rest of the night tending to Sammy's cuts and bruises because he refused to go to the emergency room. I shook my head at the memory as I unlaced my steel-toed work boot and let it drop to the floor. Then I did the same with my other boot.

"This is different, though," Sammy whispered.

I peeled Sammy's arms off my neck and pulled him around to sit next to me. I wrapped one arm around him, realizing again how frail he seemed by comparison. I cupped my free hand under his chin and tilted his head back. Then I covered Sammy's mouth with mine and tasted all that he'd had to drink as my tongue found his.

Sammy squeezed one hand under my tight-fitting black T-shirt, his slim fingers warm against my abdomen. My cock responded to the feel of his skin against mine, and by the time he unfastened my jeans and tugged down my zipper, my cock was fully erect. He wrapped his hand around it and stroked up. His fist got caught behind the spongy-soft mushroom cap, and then he massaged all the way down the root.

Suddenly, Sammy pulled his face away, breaking our kiss. He looked deep into my eyes for a moment and then slipped off the bed and knelt between my widespread thighs. I lifted my ass off the bed so that he could pull my jeans and my black low-rise jockeys down to my ankles. Burying his face in my crotch, he sucked both of my balls into his mouth and bathed them with his tongue. I kept myself shaved because Sammy didn't like to catch hair between his teeth, but it had been a few days since I'd touched up. If my ball stubble bothered Sammy, he didn't stop to mention it.

Sammy's nose pressed against the base of my erection, and his warm breath tickled almost as much as his constantly moving tongue. He still had one hand around my cock and his fist pistoned up and down as he continued bathing my balls.

"Oh, Jesus, Sammy!"

When the head of my cock glistened with drops of pre-come, Sammy knew, like he always knew, that I couldn't hold back much longer. He spit out my balls and took the head of my cock in his mouth, catching his teeth behind my swollen glans. His fist continued up and down the length of my shaft as he licked away the drops of pre-come. My hips began to buck up and down on the edge of the bed. And then I couldn't stop myself. My breath caught and my entire body stiffened when I came. I fired hot spunk against the back of Sammy's throat. He swallowed every drop, refusing to release his oral grip on my cock until it quit spasming in his mouth.

We didn't do anything else that night, and Sammy fell asleep in my arms, his head resting on my chest. While we slept, Katrina was upgraded to a category 4 hurricane and then to a category 5. We woke to find that most of the neighbors had abandoned the city. Two of them had offered us their apartment keys the night before when they'd learned that we planned to ride out the storm.

"Where would we go?" I'd asked when Sammy first broached the idea of leaving. He had no living relatives, and I might as well not have had any. My parents evicted me from their house when I came out the summer following my graduation from junior college. Like Sammy had years earlier, I drifted south, finally arriving in New Orleans. I'd been in the city for nearly a year before Sammy and I met at the club where Bordeaux performed, and he'd given me a blow job in the men's room. We crossed paths at various clubs, parties, and social events, and somewhere along the line had stopped meeting by accident and started meeting on purpose. One night, long after Sammy had healed from the bashing, he invited me to his apartment. The next morning, I moved in. I've been there ever since, taking care of Sammy and Sammy's things.

I went downstairs and secured Sammy's car in the garage. Then I locked the wrought iron gate that separated our little paradise from the hedonism of the French Quarter. An old man who lived across the street—a man so old he had probably been living in the Quarter when the Spanish took the city from the French—called to me.

"This is the big one," he said. "This one's going to fuck us all."

I returned to Sammy's apartment. He stood in the kitchen wearing only a pair of blue silk boxers, preparing eggs benedict and mimosas for our breakfast. We couldn't eat on the terrace, so we ate at the dining room table, a heavy wooden thing too big for the apartment. We could see the television in the living room, and we flipped back and forth between the cable news channels and the local stations.

"Marty called," Sammy said. Marty was the owner of the restaurant where Sammy worked as a sous chef. It was an upscale Italian restaurant, and a glance at the menu posted near the front door often sent tourists scurrying away. "He closed the restaurant. He said he's taking his family north."

"It's too late to leave," I told Sammy, pointing at the television picture of an unending line of cars crawling up Interstate 55. "We'd get stuck in that."

"We should have left with Bordeaux."

"Should have," I said. "Didn't."

Sammy shot me a look.

I held up both hands, palms toward Sammy. "Don't get pissy with me," I said. "We made the decision together."

"We made a bad decision."

"Then we'll have to make the best of it."

We filled every available container with water, including our sinks and bathtub. Then we did the same in two other apartments because we had keys. There wasn't much else we could do but wait. Sammy studied a new cookbook that he'd ordered online, and I did push-ups. He read a mystery novel, and I did sit-ups. He cleaned the kitchen, and I lifted hand weights. Later we took what turned out to be our last shower for many days. Sammy lathered my entire body and carefully shaved everything but my eyebrows. By the time he finished I was smooth as silk and my cock was hard as rock. As the water cascaded over us, I pulled him into my arms and kissed him. I kissed him hard and deep, sucking his tongue into my mouth and holding it captive until he finally resisted.

I grabbed the cheeks of Sammy's ass and pulled him tight against me, trapping my cock against his abdomen. The sparse patch of hair on his lower abdomen and the water trickling between us tickled my cock. He's shorter than me, so his rapidly stiffening cock pressed against my muscular thigh. When I shifted position slightly to rub my shaft against him, Sammy's cock head tapped against my hairless ball sac.

After I released Sammy's tongue, he kissed his way down my body. His lips caressed my neck and my chest, and he suckled each nipple in turn, drawing each one into his mouth and gently gripping it between his teeth as he massaged it with his tongue.

When my nipples were painfully hard, he dropped to his knees and my cock bobbed in his face. He kissed the head and ran the tip of his tongue all the way down the length of my shaft to my sac and then back up to the head. He cupped my balls in one hand and tickled the sensitive spot behind them with the tip of one finger as his tongue retraced its route along the underside of my shaft. He did it again, and I felt my cock begin to throb with desire.

I pulled Sammy to his feet and turned him around. Sammy bent over, bracing himself on the shower wall with one hand. I lathered my cock with soap and pressed the head against his ass. He opened to me, and soon I had my stiff shaft buried deep within him. I held his thin hips and fucked him hard. As I did that, Sammy grabbed his own cock and beat *his* stiff shaft in counter rhythm. Sammy came first, unloading a stream of come against the shower wall. Then I came with one last powerful thrust, my own hot load shooting into Sammy. We collapsed against the wall together and caught our breath before we finished our shower.

* * *

The next morning, Katrina hit the gulf coast like a dyke on the rag. But the hurricane wasn't the worst of it. Sammy woke me when the windows started to rattle. He whispered, "Hold me." We were spooning and I was behind Sammy. I pulled him into my arms and held him against my chest. I wrapped one leg over his. Before long I started stroking his hair and kissing the top of his head. My cock responded to the proximity of our bodies and grew to half-mast. Neither of us did anything about it.

For the next few days, we lived in near isolation. Without power, we had no way to hear the news. We didn't know the levees had given way and that Bordeaux's home was underwater. We didn't know about the people trapped at the Superdome or the Convention Center. All we knew is what we could see from our terrace. A small slice of the world had gone mad. During the day we heard car alarms and breaking glass. Twice we heard gunshots, close enough that we ducked inside until they stopped. One afternoon two men spotted us on the terrace. One lifted the other on his shoulders and they tried to climb up. I beat them off with a leaded glass candlestick and they staggered away bloody and bruised.

Reporters arrived, and they shouted questions up to us because we refused to leave the terrace. Were we OK? Did we need anything? How had we managed to get through the hurricane? Did we know that the levees had collapsed and that most of New Orleans had flooded? We didn't have any good answers. The

National Guard arrived. FEMA arrived. People from all over the country tried to help, but it was all too little, too late. Sammy and I should have left New Orleans with Bordeaux, but we'd chosen to ride the storm out. It had brought us closer and could so easily driven us apart.

I went back to the Hustler Club as soon as the doors opened. Marty reopened his restaurant, and Sammy resumed his work routine. Bordeaux returned without his grandparents, telling us they had stayed in Alabama with his cousin. He moved into Sammy's apartment with us because he had no home to return to.

The French Quarter has returned to life, but the Big Easy isn't so easy these days. Life here is hard for everyone, but harder on some than others. We were lucky.

Soaring

As I stared at the mirror, I adjusted my tie and straightened my uniform jacket, marveling at how much the world had changed during my years in the Air Force. Less than a year earlier I could not admit, nor could anyone ask about, my sexual orientation. Less than a year earlier I could not have married Scott and kept my commission. Less than a year earlier I could not have imagined a church filled with people about to share the moment in which Scott and I vowed eternal union.

We first met at a reception hosted by the local country club in which members wined and dined newly transferred officers, and the socially connected locals patted themselves on the back for supporting the troops. As a captain, I'd been obligated to attend and regale the attendees with heroic tales of my recent tour of duty overseas in which I'd flown several combat missions as a jet pilot but had seen far less action than the grunts on the ground. When it became obvious that I was single, I found myself fending off the attentions of several matronly women who felt certain I would be interested in their unmarried daughters.

I finally ducked into the men's room to distance myself from their attentions and have a few minutes to gather my thoughts. Even there I wasn't alone. Scott—an attractive man in his mid-thirties to whom I had been introduced at some point earlier in the evening—stood at the sink washing his hands. When he glanced in the mirror and saw me, he said, "I see the old biddies are circling you like a pack of wolves, trying to interest you in their homely and oft-divorced daughters. You don't stand a chance, Captain Hunter."

I saw that he wasn't wearing a ring. "How do you deal with it?"

"Some of them have been after me for years." He winked. "But I'm not interested in women."

Before I could respond, he stepped from the restroom and left me staring at the slowly closing door.

Scott had disappeared from the reception by the time I exited the men's room and once again attracted the circling pack of matrons. I survived the rest of the evening by repeatedly assuring the women that my duties kept me far too busy to become involved with anyone, but still they foisted off their daughters' names and phone numbers. I graciously tucked each business card and scrap of paper into my pocket but discarded them all once I returned to my quarters on base because none contained the one phone number in which I was most interested.

Scott and I didn't cross paths again until several months later. By then I was flying a desk, my daily routine kept me mostly on base, and I had resigned myself to a life of solitude and self-pleasure because I had no desire to jeopardize my military career by engaging in meaningless one-night stands. I spent many evenings with my nose in a novel and, because the PX's selection of reading material didn't coincide with my taste, I had to visit an independent bookstore off base to replenish my reading material.

While I was examining the back cover of an anthology of gay mysteries another shopper sidled up to me and said, "Captain Hunter."

When I looked up, I found Scott standing beside me.

"I almost didn't recognize you out of uniform."

I wore blue jeans, a loose-fitting sweatshirt, a baseball cap, and Ray-Ban Aviator sunglasses. I said, "That's the intent."

He glanced at the book I was holding. "That's an interesting choice for a man who was fighting women off with a stick the last time I saw him."

I shrugged and returned the paperback to the shelf. "I like mysteries."

"Don't we all," Scott said. "The biggest might be why you're shopping here."

I knew he wouldn't have to be Sherlock Holmes to figure it out, and I was right. He suggested we visit a little coffee shop around the corner to discuss his conclusion.

He ordered a cappuccino and I ordered coffee, black. We carried our cups to a booth in the back, out of sight of anyone who might glance in the front window.

We didn't mention the obvious, instead discussing our career choices—the Air Force for me, banking for him—and how they impacted our lives. I had elected to avoid most social situations that required my appearance as half of a couple while he had a pair of female friends who would beard for him on those occasions.

"I've lived here my entire life," he said, "and I learned young that discretion is the better part of valor."

"No one knows?"

"Only a small circle of trusted friends," he said, "and you. I travel frequently and attend to my needs when I'm away."

"That's a lonely way to live."

"You can get used to anything if you must."

"Even celibacy," I said.

"That bad?"

"It isn't anything I can't handle on my own," I said.

Scott laughed and reached across the table to touch my forearm. "Maybe someday we can find a solution to both our problems."

"Maybe," I agreed, but we didn't pursue the idea right then. We finished our coffee, exchanged contact information, and parted company.

Scott was first to pick up the phone when he called a few weeks later to tell me about an upcoming trip to Dallas. "Ever been?"

I admitted that I hadn't.

"Join me," he said. "I'll show you around."

*　*　*

Scott drove from Enid, and I hitched a ride in a transport plane from Vance Air Force Base, arriving a few hours after he did. I met him at a hotel where he had reserved a suite, and he took me to dinner, to the symphony, and then back to the suite where a bottle of champagne chilled in an ice bucket.

"If I didn't know better," I said, as I settled onto the couch, "I'd think you were trying to seduce me."

Scott freed the champagne bottle from the bucket, uncorked it, and filled a pair of glasses. He handed one to me and raised his in silent toast. As we sipped our champagne, he asked, "Is it working?"

"Quite well," I told him. After setting my half-empty glass on the coffee table, I reached for Scott's free hand and pulled him down on the couch beside me.

I hooked my hand behind his head, pulled his face close, and covered his lips with mine. Our first kiss was tentative and lasted only a fraction of a second. We drew a few inches apart, stared for a moment into each other's eyes as if searching for the answer to a question neither of us dared ask, and then we kissed again—deeper, harder, longer.

Scott tried to set his champagne glass on the table with mine, but he missed, and it fell to the floor. He unthreaded my tie and slipped it out of my collar. Then our fingers found buttons, buckles, and zippers, and we stripped off the suits we had worn to the symphony.

Scott kissed his way down my chest, paused for a moment to tease one of my nipples, and then continued until he reached the base of my erection. Using just the tip of his tongue, he drew a wet line along the underside of my shaft until he reached the tip of the swollen purple head. He licked away a glistening drop of pre-come before taking the first few inches of my cock into his mouth.

He wrapped one fist around my stiff shaft and pistoned his hand up and down as he hoovered my hard-on. Too much time had passed since I had last been with a man and I couldn't restrain myself. Without warning, I came, firing a thick wad of hot spunk against the back of his throat.

He swallowed and swallowed again, releasing his oral grip on me while my cock was still throbbing. He slipped off the couch, stood, and took my hand.

Then he led me into the bedroom, where we spent the next few hours exploring one another's bodies.

The following morning, we walked through Oak Lawn, a Dallas neighborhood where no one gave us a second glance when Scott took my hand. We shopped, had lunch, and shopped more. After dinner, we went club hopping, visiting three different nightclubs before we found one with the right mix of atmosphere and music to entice us onto the dance floor.

We stayed out until well past midnight and returned to our hotel suite hot, sweaty, and borderline drunk. Once the door closed behind us, I pushed Scott against the door and covered his lips with mine. I shoved my tongue into his mouth, and we kissed hard and deep and long, and by the time the kiss ended I'm certain he felt my erection prodding his thigh much as I felt his prodding mine.

As we kissed again, I unbuckled his belt, unsnapped his jeans, and drew down his zipper. I wanted Scott and I didn't want to wait. I spun him around and tugged his jeans and briefs down to his thighs.

He pushed me backward as he grabbed them before they could drop to the floor. I reached for Scott, but he spun out of my grasp and headed toward the bedroom. I followed.

He kicked off his shoes as he went, peeled off his jeans and briefs, and came to a stop on his side of the bed. He grabbed the partially used tube of lube we'd used the night before and pressed it into my hand.

I squeezed a glob onto my fingers and massaged it into his ass crack and then into his ass hole as he bent over the bed. I unfastened my own jeans and let them drop to my ankles. Then I pressed the swollen head of my erect cock along the lube-slicked crack of his ass until it pressed against the tight pucker of his sphincter.

As Scott pressed backward, I pushed forward, driving my cock deep into him. I held one hip with my left hand. My right hand was still covered with lube, so I reached around to grasp his erect cock, and I stroked it as I drew back and pushed forward.

We'd made love our first night together. Our second night, though, fueled in part by alcohol and in part by an entire day spent flirting with one another in public places where consummation of our desire might be frowned upon, we fucked and fucked hard.

I slammed into him again and again as I beat him off and Scott came first, spewing come over the bed and over my fist. I released my grip on his cock and grabbed hold of his hips with both hands. I held on tight as I drove into him several more times.

Even if I had wanted to, I couldn't have held back, and I came hard, firing hot spunk deep inside my new lover. I held him tight against me until my cock finally stopped throbbing and I could withdraw.

We stripped off the rest of our clothes and fell into bed together. I wanted to take him a second time, but the long day and the alcohol had other plans for our bodies, and we fell asleep in each other's arms.

Room service woke us when they brought breakfast Sunday morning, and I barely had time to eat after I showered and dressed. Then I shoved the last of my things into my ditty bag and grabbed my suit bag.

Scott caught me before I reached the door. He kissed me long and hard, and when the kiss ended, said, "Stay."

"I can't," I told him. "I have to return to base."

"I'll be here through the middle of the week," he said.

"You'll be in meetings all day."

"But I could devote my evenings to you," he said. "You have enjoyed the evenings, haven't you?"

"I appreciate your desire," I said, "but I have to leave."

"Can we talk when I return home?"

"There's nothing to talk about," I said. "As much as you want me and as much as I want you, we live in the same community, and we can't spend time together there."

"I'll be discreet."

I pressed a finger against his lips. "You say that now, but what will you say later? What will you say when we meet each other on the street? What will you say when you accidentally reveal my secret? I have a lot to lose, Scott. What do you have to lose?"

He didn't answer, so I opened the door and left him standing in the hotel suite. I hitched a ride home on the same cargo plane that had brought me and didn't sleep well the next few nights. I'd had my share of one-night stands and short-term relationships when I was younger, but somehow Scott had gotten under my skin in a way that no previous lover ever had. But he was out, even if only to select friends and family members, where I could not be. While I might be willing to risk my heart, I wasn't willing to risk my hard-earned military career so near to retirement.

Scott called when he returned from his trip, leaving a message on my cell phone that I didn't answer, and he called again a few days later. I was able to avoid him for nearly a month by not responding to his calls and not leaving the base, but a return visit to the country club at the insistence of my commanding officer threw us together again.

"Captain Hunter," Scott said as he thrust his hand out to clasp mine. "It's so nice to see you again. I'm surprised you were able to get away from base."

I melted inside. "I've been busy," I said, "but it looks like I'll have free time this weekend."

Before we could say any more, we were interrupted by one of the matronly women I'd met during my previous visit to the country club. This time she'd brought her daughter and she insisted on introducing us.

Scott flashed me a wicked little grin and left me to fend for myself. When I phoned later that evening, he asked if the woman had already set a wedding date for her daughter and me. I let Scott take his shot—I deserved it for the way I'd avoided him since returning from Dallas—before we began our real conversation.

We had a lot to work out, and it took more than one conversation to do it, but we soon realized we both wanted what neither of us had ever had: a relationship. And we both knew that circumstances prevented us from having a normal one. Unlike during our visit to the Oak Lawn neighborhood in Dallas, we could never hold hands in town, could never kiss in public as we had seen same-sex couples doing, and could never do anything that might circumvent the purpose of Don't Ask, Don't Tell.

We were careful, almost too careful, not sharing the same bed again until a trip to Key West three months after we met. We were so cautious and surreptitious that the announcement of our engagement a few weeks after the repeal of Don't Ask, Don't Tell caught by surprise everyone we knew.

* * *

My best man, a fellow pilot who had been less surprised by my coming out than I had expected, knocked on the door and poked his head in. "It's time."

I took one last look in the mirror and followed him to the staging area. Rather than either of us walking down the aisle, Scott and I approached the altar from either side and met in the middle. We stood before a church filled with family and friends as we professed our undying love, attended a simple reception following the ceremony, and then we drove to a hotel in the Dallas neighborhood of Oak Lawn to begin our life as a married couple.

The door of the honeymoon suite had barely closed behind the bellman when I pulled Scott into my arms and kissed him long and hard. Over the course of our developing relationship, we had kissed many times, but never like this, never as a married couple.

When the kiss ended, Scott took my hand, grabbed one of the small bags the bellman had piled just inside the door, and led me into the bedroom. As I removed my uniform and hung it in the closet, Scott unpacked the bag and stripped off his suit. Wearing only my boxers, I turned my attention to the bed, where my new spouse awaited me beneath the covers. I kicked off my boxers and joined him there.

I braced myself on one elbow and gazed down into his eyes.

"I never thought this day would come," I said as I stroked his cheek. A faint hint of five o'clock shadow sandpapered my thumb. "I never thought I could have a family *and* a military career."

I covered Scott's lips with mine before he could respond, and our kiss was longer and deeper than the one we'd shared when we'd first entered the honeymoon suite. I stroked his hair, ran my fingers down the length of his arm, cupped one ass cheek in my palm, exploring his body almost as if it were our first time together.

Scott slipped a hand between us and wrapped his fist around my rising cock, gripping it like a joystick as he thumbed the tiny slit and smeared pre-come over the spongy soft head.

Then he pushed aside the covers and kissed his way down my chest, over my taut abdomen to the neatly trimmed nest of hair at my crotch. My new spouse readjusted his position until he knelt between my widespread thighs, and his warm breath tickled the head of my cock just before he wrapped his lips around it. As he pistoned his fist up and down the stiff shaft, he covered my cock head with saliva, painting it with his tongue.

He slid his fist to the base of my cock and then took more of my length into his mouth. From past experience I knew the entire length was more than he could handle but that didn't stop him from trying.

As he drew his head back, saliva escaped and slid down the length of my shaft to dampen the thatch of hair at my crotch and tickle my ball sac. He cupped my balls with his free hand and kneaded my nuts. When his teeth caught on the ridge of my swollen glans, he reversed direction. He stopped kneading my nuts and tickled the sensitive spot behind my nut sac, his finger sliding backward until it pressed against the tight pucker of my sphincter.

He moved his head up and down, faster and faster, pressing ever more firmly against my sphincter with his unlubed finger.

I couldn't restrain myself and soon my hips were bucking up and down on the bed. I wrapped my fingers in Scott's hair and thrust upward to meet his face each time it descended.

Then, just as I was about to come, my ass relaxed, and Scott's finger slid into me and pressed against my prostate. I came and came hard, propelling a thick wad of hot spunk against the back of Scott's throat.

He swallowed every drop before he released my cock and slid up the bed into my arms. I'm not usually quick to rebound, but this was our wedding night and soon my cock rose again.

Scott had unpacked the lube while I had been undressing and it was on the nightstand. After I slathered some on my reenergized cock, I squeezed a glob on my middle fingers and slid my hands between his thighs and under his ball sac. I massaged his sphincter until I could slip one finger into Scott's ass, and I continued massaging it until I could slip in a second finger.

When I knew he was ready, I removed my fingers and rolled on top of my new spouse. I pulled his knees up until he could hook his legs over my shoulders. Then, with his erect cock trapped between us, I drove my cock into his well-lubed ass and stared into his eyes as I made love to him.

As I slowly pistoned my cock in and out of Scott's ass, my abdomen rubbed the underside of his erect cock. Our sex started slow and easy but soon grew hard and fast.

My new spouse came first, covering my abdomen and his with sticky come. Then I came, sending my second wad of hot spunk deep inside him. I collapsed atop him and didn't move until I'd caught my breath and my softening cock finally slipped free.

After we lay together for a bit, Scott said, "I'm hungry but I don't think I want to leave the bed any time soon."

"I can take care of that," I told him. I reached for the room service menu, and we examined it together. A moment later I rolled over, reached for the phone, and dialed room service. As soon as the call was answered, I said, "My husband and I would like—"

I hesitated, unexpectedly choked up. Scott and I had been married less than a day, but it was the first time I had ever referred to him as my husband. I looked over at Scott—at my husband—and felt as if I was soaring higher than I'd ever soared before without ever leaving the ground.

"Sir?" asked the voice on the other end of the line.

I kissed Scott and then completed placing our order.

My husband and I had a glorious future ahead of us.

Flyboy

Ever since I was old enough to comprehend birds, I wanted to join them. By the time I was old enough to enlist in the Air Force ROTC, I had a secret I was under no obligation to share and about which the recruiters couldn't ask, a secret that—until recently—could have grounded my military career faster than broken wings grounded the birds I envied.

Throughout college and on through a year of flight school and six months qualifying in my plane I was able to keep my secret from my fellow airmen by holding my assignations well away from campus and from the base where I was subsequently stationed. That worked until I met Terry.

A tastefully dressed slim blond, he worked for a property management company that rented houses to airmen who wanted to live off base. When we met in his office, he tried to steer me into an expensive home in an exclusive neighborhood befitting my rank, and it took some effort to convince him that I wanted a home well away from town, surrounded by plenty of undeveloped land where my private life wouldn't be subjected to prying eyes.

"Why would a handsome captain like you want to live so far from the action?" he asked as he examined me across the top of his desk, taking in my close-cropped hair, broad shoulders, and smartly tailored uniform. I kept my gaze steady, staring directly into Terry's pale blue eyes until a sly smile tugged at the corners of his mouth. Then he said, "I think I know just the place."

Terry stood and I followed him outside to his SUV, admiring the way his cute ass filled out his slacks. Thirty minutes later he led me through a fully furnished split-level well outside of town, with nary a neighboring house within sight in any direction. The decorations were sparse but tasteful, and it wasn't until we stood in the master bedroom and saw a trio of framed photographs lining the dresser—all of Terry—that I realized we were in his home.

"Are you planning to move?" I asked. By then we had stepped onto the balcony outside the bedroom and were looking across acres of undeveloped grassland. "Is that why we're here?"

"No," the rental agent said as he put one hand on my arm. "It's because I've been turned on ever since you stepped into my office this morning."

As Terry turned to face me, I was certain we were flying in the same formation. I knew better than to play in the same town where I was stationed, but months had passed since I had been with another man, and I'd been flying solo far too long. So, I didn't stop Terry when he unbuttoned my jacket, pushed it open, and placed his hand on my crotch.

Inside my uniform trousers my cock began to inflate, quickly rising to attention. As he dropped to his knees in front of me, Terry drew down the zipper and threaded my erection out through the fly front of my boxers and uniform trousers. He pushed back the foreskin to reveal the swollen purple head of my cock, and then he wrapped his lips around it.

As he hooked his teeth behind the glans, he wrapped one fist around my cock shaft and pistoned it up and down the entire length. After several strokes I pushed his hand away, wrapped my fingers in Terry's hair, and held the back of his head as I pushed my cock halfway into his mouth. I drew back and then pushed forward again and again, pushing a little deeper each time until I knew he could handle the entire length.

I hadn't left base that morning anticipating a hookup and would never have intentionally sought one out so close to where I was stationed, yet I found myself with my cock in Terry's mouth, enjoying the feel of his tongue and his teeth on my tumescent member. And I never would have thought myself capable of having an encounter in so public a place as the balcony of someone's home, yet I hadn't stopped Terry when he'd dropped to his knees before me, and I certainly had no intention of stopping him after he'd taken me into his mouth.

I drew back and pushed forward, my pace quickening as orgasm drew near. Before I could stop myself, my sac tightened and I came, firing thick wads of hot spunk against the back of Terry's throat. He swallowed as fast as he could, but not fast enough and some of my come dripped down his chin. After my cock ceased spasming, I stepped back, pulled it from his mouth, and tucked it away. Terry wiped at his chin with the back of his hand and looked up at me. The metal teeth of my zipper had scratched his nose, but he didn't seem to notice. I grabbed his hand, pulled him to his feet, and together we stepped inside.

"You do this for all your clients?"

"Only special clients," he said with a smile.

We returned to his office and from there, after assurances that Terry would continue looking for an appropriate rental home, I returned to my quarters on the base. I wasn't sure how I felt about what had happened at Terry's house, but I was kept busy the next few days and I didn't have time to give it much thought.

Later that week Terry found a rental house for me a few miles farther down the road, one with a driveway that looped around the house to the garage in back. For the next few years, we kept our developing relationship as much a secret as possible, spending all our time at his home or mine and never being seen together in public unless we were far from the base.

Tuesday, September 20, 2011, changed our relationship forever with the repeal of Don't Ask, Don't Tell. I'd not seen the news that day, so I was surprised when I returned home from the base that evening to find Terry waiting in my living room, wearing his best suit.

"Change clothes," he said. "We have dinner reservations."

After Terry told me what we were celebrating, I changed from fatigues into my dress blues and we drove downtown to an Italian restaurant with valet parking, inflated prices, and an impressive wine selection.

We started with wine, toasting our good fortune and the good fortune of so many of my brothers and sisters silently serving in the armed forces.

While waiting for our appetizers to arrive, Terry reached across the table and took my hand. After years of hiding our relationship, my instinct was to pull away, but Terry wouldn't let me. He held on fast.

"We don't have to hide anymore."

I glanced around the restaurant, expecting to be the center of attention, but no one was paying any attention to us. I relaxed, took another sip of wine, and stared into Terry's pale-blue eyes much as I had the first time we'd met. I knew exactly what he saw when he looked at me, because I saw the same thing when I looked at him.

Our appetizers came, followed in due time by dinner, a dessert we shared, and more than one glass of wine. Perhaps we shouldn't have driven home under the influence of all that wine, but we made it without incident.

As soon as we stepped through the back door, we were all over each other, kissing and groping and stripping off our clothes as we made our way to my bedroom. A trail of abandoned clothing followed us, the last of it landing in a heap next to the bed.

I pulled Terry to me and kissed him hard, my tongue thrust deep into his mouth. When the kiss ended, I spun him around and bent him forward. He braced himself on the bed while I grabbed a tube of lube from the nightstand.

After slathering lube over my tumescent cock, I squeezed a glob into my lover's ass crack. I massaged it into the tight pucker of his ass hole until I was able to ease my middle finger into him.

Then I pulled my finger away and pressed my fat cock head against his sphincter. I grabbed his hips as he slowly opened to me, but I was impatient and pushed hard, driving myself deep inside him.

Keeping a tight grip on his hips, I drew back and pressed forward, pumping hard and fast until I couldn't restrain myself. I came, and came hard, driving into him one last time before firing a thick wad of hot spunk deep into Terry's ass.

I held him until my cock finally stopped throbbing and I could pull myself free. Then we collapsed on the bed, and I held him in my arms.

"This is the day we've been waiting for," Terry said.

I kissed him before he could say any more. He was right, but did I have the courage to follow through on my promise to marry him now that a public revelation of our relationship wouldn't ground me? Terry had willingly played second fiddle to my career but now he didn't have to.

"Tomorrow," I whispered. "Tomorrow we'll tell everyone."

* * *

The next day I spoke to some of my fellow pilots, letting word-of-mouth carry the news to everyone on base who mattered. Some of my fellow airmen claimed they'd known which way I flew but hadn't said anything. Others appeared surprised by the news.

Over the next several weeks a handful of other officers and more than a dozen enlisted personnel also came out. None, however, came out by announcing their impending wedding as I had done.

We didn't rush the wedding, but waited until the following January to tie the knot before our closest friends and family. Then we attended a reception at the Officers' Club, thrown in our honor by like-minded airmen.

As Terry and I walked hand-in-hand into the club, publicly acknowledging our relationship in a way we could not have less than a year earlier, I felt as if I were soaring.

I lifted my wine glass and toasted my ten-year companion, a man I had met while completing graduate studies in English literature at a private university in Texas. We dated for a year before committing to one another, but marriages and civil unions didn't exist back then—and still don't in Texas—so we celebrated our anniversary on the day Daryl moved into my one-bedroom apartment. The ink was still wet on my diploma, I had just accepted a position teaching bonehead English at a community college, and we had no idea what a life together would entail.

The evening we met, Daryl was slinging drinks at a chain restaurant where all the employees were encouraged to cover their shirts with bling, and only a handful of drinkers occupied the bar. The first time I saw him he was bent over behind the bar retrieving a dropped towel, his black slacks stretched tight across his firm ass. I made some appreciative comment to my drinking companion—a lipstick lesbian who had asked me to beard for her at a dinner meeting earlier that Friday evening and who was picking up the tab that night—and she just shrugged. Her eye was on a rail-thin undergrad sitting alone in a back booth, a bottle of Shiner Bock at her elbow and a copy of *Madame Bovary* open on the table before her.

When Daryl straightened and turned to take our drink orders, I was smitten. His warm smile and glittering emerald eyes captivated me in a way that I had not previously experienced, and I felt my pulse race.

Anita ordered a Cosmopolitan, but I kept it simple. After Daryl placed her Cosmopolitan and my Jack and Coke in front of us, my companion slid her Visa card across the bar, told Daryl to run a tab for both of us, and asked for a bottle of Shiner. He returned a moment later with her card and the Shiner.

My companion slid off the barstool and carried her drinks to the back booth where the rail-thin undergrad looked up, listened, and then closed her book. Anita slid into the booth opposite her and pushed the opened Shiner across the table.

Daryl said, "Looks like your friend has her own agenda this evening."

I shrugged. "We don't play on the same team."

He leaned against the bar and placed his hand on my forearm. I could feel the weight of it through my jacket sleeve. Still gazing into my eyes, Daryl lowered his voice and asked, "What team do you play for?"

Daryl later told me he knew the answer long before he asked the question, having once seen me in the company of a mutual friend, and we were still talking when Anita left with the undergrad.

"There goes my ride," I told Daryl when the two women walked out the front door. "I might need you to call me a cab."

"If you don't mind waiting until closing," he suggested with a wink, "I can give you a ride."

I smiled and loosened my tie. I didn't mind a bit.

Less than an hour passed before last call, and soon I was sitting in the passenger seat of Daryl's Toyota, giving him directions to the apartment complex where my one-bedroom apartment was directly over the laundry room and often smelled of detergent and dirty clothes.

I invited him upstairs for a nightcap, but we both knew it was only an excuse to get him in my apartment, and I barely had the door closed behind us before we were in each other's arms. I had removed my tie during the ride and my jacket on the walk up the stairs. So, I dropped them to the floor, pushed Daryl back against the door, and covered his mouth with mine.

He smelled of sweat and aftershave and alcohol but tasted of peppermint when our tongues met, as if he had sucked on one of the after-dinner mints the restaurant kept in a bowl by the exit. Our kisses were deep and hard, threatening to take my breath away. His turgid cock tented the front of his slacks and jabbed at me through our clothing. Mine did the same in return.

Our hands fumbled with buttons. I pulled his shirt free of his waistband and pushed it from his shoulders. It slid down his muscular arms and dropped to our feet, the bling clanking against the linoleum foyer floor. He wore a V-neck T beneath the shirt, and I pulled it off him, finally revealing his thick, hairless chest and washboard abs.

My voice husky with desire, I told him how much I wanted him right then. "Don't make me wait."

Daryl grabbed my belt buckle. In a split second he had my pants around my ankles and was on his knees in front of me. I hadn't groomed because I had not expected an evening spent bearding for a lipstick lesbian to lead to a night of carnal delight, but the dark crotch forest didn't seem to bother Daryl.

He wrapped one fist around my cock, his thumb and forefinger tightly encircling the shaft just below the mushroom cap of my cock head. I felt an unexpected rush of pain and pleasure that only increased when he bent forward and drew the head of my cock between his lips. He hooked his teeth behind my swollen purple cock head and painted it with broad tongue strokes, licking away the drops of pre-come that oozed out as his fist pumped up and down my shaft.

He grabbed my scrotum with his free hand and kneaded my balls, keeping both of his hands busy as he worked me ever closer to orgasm. My hips began to thrust forward and back, but Daryl never took more the head of my cock in his mouth that first time. Before long, my balls began to tighten. I knew I couldn't restrain myself and I didn't try.

I came and came hard, firing a thick stream of warm spunk into Daryl's mouth. As I came, he squeezed my balls together so that I felt concurrent pleasure and pain. My eyelids fluttered and closed, and I had to press one hand against the door to support myself until my cock stopped spasming in Daryl's mouth.

When it did, he unwrapped his lips from my cock head, released his vise grip on my scrotum, and stood. As he held my head between his hands and planted an open-mouth kiss on me, Daryl used his tongue to push a ball of my own come into my mouth, surprising me. No one had ever done that before, and I swallowed without thinking.

We stripped off the rest of our clothes, leaving a trail of discarded fabric from the front door of my apartment to the bed. I opened a new tube of lube that night, and I don't think we fell asleep until the sun began to peek through the curtains.

* * *

As we touched our wine glasses, I asked Daryl if he remembered that first night as well as I did.

"How could I forget?" he replied with a wicked smile and a gleam in his eye. "You were an insatiable dream come true. We didn't get out of your bed until you had to leave for class Monday morning."

Despite a four-year age difference and a significant gap in education level, our relationship developed rapidly after that night. Soon Daryl and I found ourselves together more often than not, and even though lust brought us together, we discovered many mutual interests outside the bedroom.

"Remember what happened the night I moved in?" Daryl asked.

"Of course." My cock had grown hard remembering our first night together, but now it became a steel beam in my pants, and I was thankful that the white tablecloth hid the physical evidence of my lust-filled memories of our ten years together.

Even though I had asked Daryl to move in and he had agreed nearly two months before his lease expired, we waited until the day after I graduated—the last day on his lease—to move most of his things. By the time we schlepped all his stuff from his apartment to my second-floor walk-up, we had killed the entire day, had turned my apartment into a maze of poorly packed boxes and duplicate furniture, and were sweating like day laborers. The temperature outside had toyed with triple digits all afternoon and we had stripped down to cut-offs and running shoes.

We should have been tired after a day filled with serious physical exertion, but we were jazzed by the idea of finally living together, of not having to wonder which apartment housed our hiking boots, our favorite shirt, or that frozen pizza we planned to have for dinner. We were looking forward to waking each morning and not having one of us slip out early to return home.

I surprised Daryl with a bottle of champagne I had chilled to celebrate the moment, and Daryl popped the cork after he carried in the last box of his stuff. The plastic cork bounced off the kitchen ceiling and three cardboard boxes before coming to a rest under the kitchen table, and champagne sprayed my chest before Daryl turned the bottle toward the sink. I caught as much of the spillage as I could in a pair of champagne glasses, and then Daryl set the bottle on the counter.

"To us," I toasted. And then, stealing a line from our favorite old television series, added, "May we live long and prosper."

Thirstier than we'd thought, we downed the champagne without hesitation. Then Daryl decided he hadn't had enough and began licking the spilled champagne from my chest. He didn't just lick away the champagne. He also sucked my nipples, bringing them to life and causing my cock to quickly rise to attention.

"I hope you realize what you started," I whispered hoarsely as I pushed him away.

"You think you're up to it?"

I reached out for him, but Daryl twisted away.

"You'll have to catch me."

There really wasn't anywhere to run, but he managed to elude my grasp by dodging around the boxes that surrounded the kitchen table and were stacked throughout the living room. I finally caught him in the bedroom, where his box spring and mattress leaned against the wall. We kicked off our running shoes and stripped away our cut-offs, revealing erections throbbing with anticipation. He'd teased me enough and I was impatient. I grabbed Daryl's wrist and spun him around, face into the mattress leaning against the wall. I grabbed a tube of lube from the nightstand, slathered it over my cock, and then took him from behind.

My slickened cock head pressed against the tight pucker of his ass and Daryl pushed back against me. Then he opened up and I buried my cock deep inside him. I drew back and pressed forward.

I reached around and took Daryl's cock in my hand, my fist trapped between his mattress and his taut abdomen, and pumped my fist up and down twice as fast as I pumped my cock into his ass. He came first, spewing spunk all over my fist, his abdomen, and the mattress. His knees went wobbly, and I grabbed his hips to steady him, my own pumping growing faster and harder until I couldn't hold back any longer.

With one last, firm thrust, I drove my cock deep inside Daryl, pressing him tight against the mattress as I emptied my balls inside his ass.

We leaned against that mattress for the longest time, neither of us wanting to step away and end the moment. We had just consummated our couplehood, the closest thing to a wedding night we were likely to get.

But I had one surprise left. When I finally pulled away from Daryl and he turned to face me, I reached into the nightstand and retrieved a pair of gold bands I had purchased earlier that week.

We've been wearing them ever since.

Throughout the rest of our ten-year anniversary dinner, we reminisced about other memorable couplings, including the time he'd blown me in a movie theater while watching a movie so bad we were the only people there, and the time we'd done it on a Florida beach during one of our summer vacations. By the time we finished our meal and left the restaurant, both our cocks were straining for release. We'd gotten a little old to be doing it in a parking lot, so I headed straight home.

On the ride, Daryl asked, "Whatever happened to Anita?"

"The last time I heard from her," I said as I pulled into the driveway of our home, "she was writing PR copy for a beer company in St. Louis and had finally met the love of her life."

Then we went inside and made another memory.

I discovered a gray hair on Gary's chest this morning when I woke wrapped in his arms. As I stared at it, I realized how much time had passed since I had first run my fingers through his chest hair.

We met as undergraduates at the University of Texas at Austin while George W. Bush was stumbling his way through his first year in the presidency. We weren't interested in Bush—in our bed or in our White House—much to the dismay of our fundamentalist parents, though mine ultimately proved more accepting of our relationship than Gary's. We were a pair of small-town boys who'd had to go along to get along through high school, even though we'd had no interest in feeling up the cheerleaders or banging the Homecoming Queen, and academics provided our escape from the confines of Southern Baptist narrow-mindedness. We'd reached the university from different Central Texas towns that were far more alike than their zip codes indicated and didn't meet one another until fall of our senior year when we were a government major and an English major rolling burritos at a popular restaurant for the pocket change entry-level employment provided.

Gary, who wore his coal-black hair trimmed close to the scalp and who seemed unable to banish the permanent five o'clock shadow on his square jaw and strong chin, had played six-man football in high school. Three years later he retained the thick, muscular body of a football linesman. Though I often glanced at his firm ass and the bulging package accentuated by his tight-fitting jeans, I avoided displaying any obvious interest. My gaydar had proven woefully inadequate throughout my first three years at the university, and I'd had to talk my way out of too many embarrassing and potentially dangerous situations since moving to Austin.

I had been editor of my high school's newspaper, had been on the yearbook staff, and had avoided all extracurricular physical activities until my sophomore year of college when I discovered RecSports. I dropped my freshman fifteen through a combination of swimming and weight training, and with continued use of the university's recreational facilities, had toned and sculpted my body so that I was no longer the pudgy kid who'd graduated valedictorian. Even so, I retained a mental self-image of that pudgy kid, worried no one would be attracted to me, until those occasions when I caught a glimpse of my reflection and realized how much my body had changed during the intervening years.

My first three weeks on the job, Gary and I often worked the same shift behind the counter, rolling burritos for a never-ending stream of customers at the popular downtown restaurant that employed us. Our conversation, limited as it was, never became personal, so I had no reason to think he was interested in me until we were walking out of the restaurant at the end of our shift one Saturday night.

The restaurant had closed at midnight, and it had taken almost half an hour for employees to clean up, clock out, and make our way out the back door. I had just reached my car and opened the door when Gary called to me.

"Dwayne?" He pronounced my name as a single syllable, not as two syllables the way my family and friends did back home.

I turned.

"Can I hitch a ride?" He explained that his car was in the shop after a fender bender with a clueless coed who'd been talking to her passenger when she plowed her car into the back of his at a stoplight near campus.

"Sure."

I climbed into the driver's seat and then reached across to unlock the passenger door. Gary climbed in beside me, provided directions, and less than ten minutes later I pulled my car into his apartment building's parking lot.

"You in a hurry?" he asked.

I shook my head.

"Want to come up for a beer?"

I had no other plans, so I found an empty parking spot and pulled my car into it. Then I followed Gary into the building and upstairs to his second-floor apartment, a one-bedroom much nicer than the exterior of the building suggested it would be.

He led me into the kitchen, opened two bottles of Lone Star beer he retrieved from the fridge, and handed one to me. As I pressed the bottle to my lips and tilted it upward to take my first drink, Gary said, "I've seen you sneaking glances at my ass."

I quickly swallowed so that I wouldn't spit out my beer. I started to sputter a protest as I lowered the bottle from my lips.

He stopped me. "It's okay," he said. "I've noticed yours, too."

My cock twitched in my pants when I realized where Gary was headed with his comments. "You didn't invite me up here just to drink a couple of beers, did you?"

Gary put his Lone Star on the kitchen counter, stepped forward, and began unbuttoning my shirt from the top. By the time he pulled it free of my jeans and unfastened the final button, my cock had swollen with desire and pressed against the inside of my Jockey shorts, yearning to be free. When Gary pushed my shirt off my shoulders, I set my bottle on the counter next to his and let my shirt slide down my arms to pool on the kitchen floor at my feet.

I wore no undershirt and Gary must have liked what he saw. He took my hand and led me from the kitchen to the bedroom, where we undressed each other. The only light illuminating the room came from a streetlight half a block away, but it was enough for me to appreciate the naked man standing before me.

Gary's perpetual five o'clock shadow should have been a clue, but I hadn't realized how hirsute he would be. Dark hair covered his chest, tapering to a treasure trail down his taut abdomen that led to a wild tangle of black pubic hair from which rose a cock thicker and longer than any I'd ever before encountered.

I couldn't believe my luck as I reached out and ran my fingers through his chest hair. Gary was everything I had ever imagined, and more. I'd dreamed about this moment, had toyed with myself in the shower while imagining various encounters with Gary, but had never expected to find myself in his bedroom. I had never been so aroused in my life, and my cock throbbed with desire and anticipation.

He reached for my erection and wrapped his fist around it. Before he could do anything else, I came, covering his hand with my sexual effluent.

We still laugh about it all these years later, but it wasn't so funny then. I was mortified. "I—I'm sorry," I stuttered. "I've never—this has never—"

"It's okay," Gary said as he released his hold on my rapidly deflating cock.

I'd fooled around with several guys but had never progressed beyond mutual masturbation and blowjobs. They had been meaningless romps for no reason beyond simply getting each other off. Being with Gary was different. I had lusted after him for weeks, but more than that, he wanted more than a quick hand job.

He had a partially used tube of lube and a selection of lubricated condoms in his nightstand drawer. After he spun me around and had me bend over his bed, he slathered lube and my ejaculate into my ass crack. Then he opened one of the condoms and slipped it over his thick cock.

He stroked my sphincter until I relaxed enough that he could slip one lube-covered finger into me. After a few probing strokes, he removed his finger and replaced it with the head of his condom-covered cock, pressing firmly until I opened to him. He must have known he was fucking a virgin ass because he carefully eased into me until his entire length was buried in my shit chute. I sighed with pleasure.

Gary grabbed my hips and drew back until only his cock head remained inside me. Then he pushed forward again. He started slowly but moved faster and faster until he was pistoning into my ass with increasing speed and power. My flaccid cock slapped against my thigh with each of his powerful thrusts until I cupped my hand over it, and I felt my come-covered cock head paint my palm as it bounced in rhythm to Gary's pistoning.

My cock was just beginning to recover from my initial orgasm and was again swelling with desire when Gary came. He slammed into me one last time, moaning with pleasure as he held my hips tight against him and filled the condom with come.

He didn't withdraw until his cock stopped spasming. When he did finally step back, he pinched the condom against the base of his cock so that it would not slip off as he withdrew. I turned, sat on the side of his bed, and watched as he walked naked down the hall to the bathroom, admiring his tight ass and powerful legs. I heard water run for a moment and he soon returned with our beers but sans condom.

Still embarrassed from my premature ejaculation, I wasn't sure what to say. So, I drank my beer, pulled on my clothes, and told Gary I had to be going. He walked me to his apartment door without bothering to dress and he leaned against the open door when I stepped into the hall.

"See you at work?" he said.

"Yeah," I said. I couldn't look into his eyes, instead focusing on the thick cock that had been inside me only a short time earlier. I wondered if I would ever see it again. "Monday. My next shift is Monday."

As I drove away a few minutes later, I didn't know if our encounter was going to be a one-time hookup or if it would lead to something more. At home in the shower, my hand wrapped around my rejuvenated cock, I imagined future encounters.

During our shift Monday evening Gary made it clear that he wanted more, and the following weekend we had a proper date. His car had just come from the shop, so he picked me up and we went to a bar he knew on Sixth Street where we could dance and drink without being harassed.

Gary danced with me, held my hand, and kissed me without hesitation, treating me as his lover and not his hookup for the evening. He introduced me to several other men at the bar, making it clear to me that he was a regular as well as that I was taken. I'd never had any of my previous sexual playmates treat me as anything more than a fuck buddy or worse, as someone for late night assignations but not someone to associate with in the cold light of day. Gary made me feel special in a way no one else ever had.

Late that evening Gary took me back to his place. I didn't embarrass myself a second time, and I fell asleep in his arms after an abundance of mutual satisfaction.

That was only the beginning of our whirlwind relationship. By the end of the semester, I was spending more nights in Gary's apartment than in my own, and our relationship, though it had started with a sexual encounter, developed into much more. After graduation we remained in Austin, choosing to cohabitate in the blue heart of a red state. Gary took an entry-level job working for the State of Texas while I found a position as assistant to the advertising director of a performing arts organization. During subsequent years I was promoted to advertising director and Gary had a meteoric rise through a series of government positions with increasing responsibility and commensurate pay.

Much like every couple that remains together for more than a dozen years, Gary and I went through several ups and down in our relationship—from financial struggles created primarily by crippling student loans to dealing with his family's complete rejection of him after we purchased a downtown loft together and they realized he wasn't just going through a phase. My parents grudgingly accepted Gary but made it clear they did not approve of our relationship. We found ways to survive the downs, making the ups even better, and along the way we found our place in the community.

We were social creatures, made friends easily, and turned our loft into a gathering place for the capital's up-and-comers. Our dinner parties brought artistic aesthetes and government wonks together in ways neither of us could ever have imagined growing up in small Texas towns, and everyone in the know desired invitations to our holiday cocktail parties.

Despite multiple opportunities to stray—he with interns looking to curry favors and me with touring performers seeking little more than one-night stands—we remained true to one another, one of the core values we had learned from our families. Sometimes we told each other about the advances others made—from the most awkward to the most subtle—and used them to spice up our bedroom play, and sometimes we kept them to ourselves to fuel our own fantasies.

We still can't marry in Texas, but our relationship was as committed as any marriage in every way but legal. We had done all we could to let the world know we were a committed couple. What was mine was Gary's and what was Gary's was mine, with joint checking and saving accounts, joint ownership of the loft and both cars, and each other named as beneficiaries on our life insurance policies. Some of the things we did to cement our relationship were things we learned from our parents, while other things we learned by watching the mistakes of our friends, many of whom ran through relationships like water through cheesecloth.

We settled into our early thirties confident in our careers and our social status but no longer the hot-bodied young men we had been when we met. The years had softened us both, but we still saw each other through lovers' eyes—a gaze that tightens flab and softens wrinkles, especially when we fail to wear our glasses or put in our contact lenses. Even so, I couldn't avoid the reality of the single strand of gray hair only inches from my nose.

As my lover snored lightly, I wondered what else might have gone gray. I pushed back the sheet covering us both and repositioned myself so that I could examine the neatly trimmed black pubic hair nestling his cock and ball sac. I soon found another gray hair spiraling outward from his left testicle.

Without my glasses, I had to get quite close to his crotch to see it and my warm breath must have tickled Gary's fancy. His flaccid cock twitched and began to rise, just as long and thick and magnificent as it had ever been.

I couldn't help myself. I wrapped my fist around the base of Gary's erect cock and took his swollen purple cock head between my lips. I pistoned my fist up and down his stiff shaft as I traced the circumference of his glans with the tip of my tongue. Before long, my lover moaned softly and shifted position ever so slightly.

I knew Gary was waking when I felt one hand on the back of my head and the other on my shoulder. I released my grip on his cock shaft and slowly drew the entire length of his cock into my mouth, something I had not been able to do when we first met. Then I drew back, stopping only when my teeth caught on the ridge of his swollen glans.

As I lowered my face to his crotch, I cupped his ball sac in the palm of my hand, covering the telltale gray hair. I massaged his testicles as my face continued bobbing up and down the entire length of his cock shaft, and I tasted the first drops of pre-come.

My saliva and his pre-come dampened his pubic hair and slid around his ball sac to his ass crack. As I massaged his scrotum in my palm, I teased his sphincter with the tip of my index finger.

Soon Gary began bucking his hips up and down, thrusting upward to meet my descending face, and I knew he would soon come. When I suspected he was close, I pressed my finger hard against his saliva-slickened sphincter, pushing my finger in his ass up to the second knuckle as he cried out and came in my mouth.

I swallowed and swallowed again, and I held his cock in my mouth until it finally quit spasming and began to contract to its flaccid state. After I released my oral grip on my lover, I returned to the position I'd been in before I'd spotted his gray chest hair: his arms.

Gary stroked my hair and asked what had prompted me to rouse him from sleep the way I had.

I told him about the gray hair, how it had made me think of how young we'd been when we'd met, and how those thoughts had reminded me of everything we had shared during our time together.

"It's not the first gray hair," Gary said when I finished. "I've been pulling them out for weeks, hoping you'd never notice. If I had known this would be the result, I might never have pulled them out."

"Don't pull out anymore," I told him as I looked into his eyes, seeing both the young man I had fallen for so many years before and the man who still made my heart beat fast. "Let me love you as you are."

Maryjane: Then and Now

"Wear the uniform again, Tommy." Stephen lay on the bed, a thin sheet his only cover, watching me rummage through the closet. "You know I love the uniform."

The last time I had worn my uniform I'd barely been able to button my shirt and fasten my pants, and I'd done little since then to rein in my once-taut abdomen. "Not now."

"Why not, Tommy? Why not wear it for me?"

"Maybe tonight," I repeated. I selected a short-sleeved, green-and-white-striped seersucker shirt, tan chinos, and a pair of brown cap-toe oxfords, and I dressed in front of the open closet while Stephen continued to watch me, and I remembered the day we'd met.

* * *

I had just returned from Vietnam, having served my time without being outed, and I was only a few days away from discharge when we met. Fresh from the Ft. Hood barber, my black hair cut high and tight, I wore my uniform—all razor-sharp creases and mirror-polished boots—to visit friends in Austin who took me to a house party where my uniform brought sideways glances and caused some attendees to vacate any room I entered.

Stephen, a draft-dodging undergraduate at the University of Texas, wore faded purple bell-bottom hip-huggers, a colorful dashiki, love beads, and leather sandals. He'd parted his blond hair in the middle, and it hung plumb straight to his shoulders. The only thing we seemed to have in common was the haze of marijuana smoke that enveloped us.

I had smoked my first doobie in-country, sharing it with an Alabama redneck so white he glowed in the dark, and a coal-black Chicagoan, the three of us unlikely to ever meet if it weren't for the draft, our insignificant high school GPAs, and our parents' low socioeconomic standings.

"The poor are always canon fodder in a rich man's war," I told Stephen as I passed him the doobie a braless brunette had handed me few minutes earlier.

"For sure," he said, already several tokes beyond the ability to hold rational conversation. He said, "That's righteous thinking, man." Then he drew a long drag, held the smoke in his lungs, and passed the doobie back to me. Only the roach remained so I ate it.

I don't know where my friends had disappeared to by then, but I didn't care. Stephen was stroking my thigh and telling me how groovy I looked in my uniform. As my cock lengthened and stiffened, I realized that we had more in common than a relationship with Maryjane.

Then Stephen decided he was hungry. He braced himself on my shoulder and pushed himself to his feet. After I stood, he took my hand and led me into the kitchen, where a random assortment of snack foods had been spread across the counter. He pawed through everything until he found an unopened bag of Chips Ahoy!

"Far out," he said when he showed the package to me. He stuck it under his dashiki and led me out of the kitchen. Our next stop was an upstairs bedroom in the back of the house, and we sat on the floor with our backs to the bed, staring out the sliding glass door and down at the backyard as we devoured every chocolate chip cookie in the bag. Stephen even licked the cookie dust off the inside of the bag, and I thought he looked so funny I laughed until I blew snot out of my nose.

"You're cool, man," Stephen said as I wiped my nose with the back of my hand. "You're like, what, a colonel or something, right?"

I had never been anything more than a private, had never aspired to be anything more than a private, had wanted only to serve my time in-country and get the hell out, and I told him so.

"Private?" he said. "I like privates. They take orders, don't they, colonel?" He patted his pockets and said he wished he had another smoke, something he could put in his mouth and suck on. Finding nothing in his own pockets, he began patting my pockets, and my cock responded to his touch. Stephen noticed. He stopped patting my pockets and concentrated on my crotch. "What do you have in there, soldier boy?" He unzipped my trousers, reached through my government-issue boxers, and wrapped his fist around my tumescent cock. He pulled it free of the confining material and then buried his face in my lap. I couldn't see what he was doing because his long blond hair blocked my view, but I could certainly feel it when he wrapped his lips around the swollen head of my cock.

I'd not had a man's mouth around my cock since a brief encounter in a San Francisco bathhouse during a two-day layover on my way to Nam, and I couldn't restrain myself. Stephen had barely taken half my length into his mouth when I came, firing a thick wad of hot spunk against the back of his throat.

He swallowed and then licked my softening cock clean before he pulled away. He patted my thigh before he stood up and said, "Wait here, I'll be back in a minute."

I tucked my cock back inside my government-issue boxers, zipped my fly closed, and waited. In the backyard two women had removed their tops and one of the men had removed all his clothes. They and half a dozen others danced to music that had no discernable beat.

Stephen returned with two bottles of Lone Star beer, a container of Crisco cold from the refrigerator, and another doobie. He popped open both beer bottles and handed one to me. Then he snuggled up next to me and lit the doobie. We passed it back and forth between swallows of beer.

"You were there, man," he said, "and, like, what were you fighting for?"

"My life," I told him. The Vietnamese didn't want us there and we didn't want to be there and every day in-country made me more aware of my own mortality. The Alabama redneck had his face blown off by a sniper when he was standing so close that bits of his brain splattered my face, and the Chicagoan had his throat slit during his turn at watch while I slept next to him in the same foxhole. In the backyard one of the girls wrapped an American flag around her shoulders and I said I fought so she could do that.

Stephen followed my gaze. "So, why'd you go, colonel?"

"I didn't have a choice."

"Everybody has a choice, man." He put one hand in my lap. "Canada's a choice."

"Nobody from my small town ever went to Canada, not before me and not after me."

"A bunch of good little privates, huh, colonel?"

"Cannon fodder," I said. "Nothing but cannon fodder."

We finished the doobie and Stephen popped the roach into his mouth. Then he twisted around and kissed me hard, his tongue found mine, and before I realized it, I had the roach in my mouth. I swallowed.

I had unbuttoned my jacket when we were in the living room, so it was easy for Stephen to unthread my tie and unbutton my shirt. I pulled the dashiki over his head as he kicked off his sandals. He peeled his purpled hip-huggers off and wasn't wearing anything beneath them. By then my cock stood at attention, a good little soldier surprisingly ready for action so soon after his first encounter with an opposing force, and Stephen helped me shed the rest of my clothes until he wore only his love beads, and I wore only my dog tags.

He opened the Crisco, scooped out a fistful, and slathered some of the still-cold shortening on my cock, causing it to temporarily lose rigidity. He reached beneath his erect cock and between his legs and smeared some Crisco up the crack of his ass.

"You've wanted me ever since we met," Stephen said as he turned his back to me. I had, and I grabbed his hips. I pressed the head of my shortening-covered cock against his sphincter and pressed forward. Maryjane had relaxed Stephen and I entered him with minimal resistance.

I pressed my entire length into his ass and then drew back, pressed forward and drew back again. As I fucked Stephen, he wrapped his Crisco-covered fist around his own cock and pumped hard and fast. He came first, firing a stream of come across the jumbled pile of our clothing, leaving a stain on my uniform jacket that I would pay hell explaining if my sergeant saw it before I had my jacket cleaned.

At that precise moment, though, I didn't care. I drew back and pushed forward, pumping harder and faster until I was slamming into Stephen's ass, my desire compounded by a year spent hiding my true sexual desires from the cooze hounds of my platoon and confused with my anger at returning home to a country where the people I thought I had been defending were spitting on my uniform. His love beads bounced against his chest while my metal dog tags jangled against mine. I wasn't just having sex with Stephen; I was fucking everything he represented, from draft-dodging college students to country club politicians who sent poor kids to fight their battles while their own sons played solider in National Guard units.

And when I came, I came hard, slamming into Stephen with enough power to knock him off balance, and I fired wad after wad of hot spunk into his ass as we collapsed on the bed.

We've been together ever since; what binds us together more powerful than anything that might have driven us apart.

* * *

We are old men now, Vietnam a distant memory, cancer our newfound enemy, and one friend from those days still welcome in our home. When I returned that evening, I put on my uniform, leaving one shirt button unfastened over my abdomen, and sat on the bed next to Stephen. I rolled a doobie from the lid I'd purchased while I was away, lit it, and passed it to him.

The first toke began to take away his pain.

Let Us Go Down to the Sea

I worked behind the bar at McGinty's, pouring drafts and opening bottles for hardworking men fresh off the boats and for tourists seeking authentic dockside experiences. The place had been in continuous operation since the late 1800s, with modern conveniences such as electricity, indoor plumbing, and pressurized beer dispensers added over the years. The years had been good to me as well, but though I'd matured from delicate to wiry, I remained too short to look most men in the eye.

There were a few rooms on the second floor, but the only one still furnished was a one-room efficiency where Peg-Leg Pete had lived before his daughters moved him to a nursing home. When one of our regulars had too much to drink, I would walk him upstairs to Pete's room and let him sleep it off. Sometimes I even crashed there myself, remembering the nights when we were young that I had spent in Pete's arms.

At the front of the building, over the entrance to the bar, Pete's room faced the harbor, and anyone standing at the window could watch the fishing boats leave each morning and return each evening. Pete had often done just that, and he never failed to keep me apprised of the comings and goings of all the vessels in the harbor, from the working craft for which it was their home port to the pleasure craft that occasionally visited. We often joked that Pete was waiting for his ship to come in, but little did I know that he wouldn't be watching the harbor when it did.

The Veterans Administration would probably have helped Pete obtain a prosthetic limb, but he would have none of it and pshawed anyone who made the suggestion. His wooden leg, the eye patch he sometimes wore over his left eye and sometimes wore over his right, his grizzled mug with its permanent three-day growth of gray stubble, and his oft-told tale of losing the bottom half of his left leg to a great white shark that rivaled anything Peter Benchley ever created, had tourists lining up to buy his beer. The fact that he could see perfectly well out of both eyes and that he'd actually lost his leg when it caught in a cable being drawn in by a purse-line winch while working on an American seiner in 1951, didn't slow him down any. His tale of battling the shark just grew as the years passed.

I missed Pete after his daughters had him taken to the home, and I visited when I could. I sat with him, held his hand, and shared whatever dockside gossip I had heard in the bar that week. I didn't know if he heard me or even knew I was there, but it comforted me to know that he might. He had been the only man I ever loved in a community where one could never express that love in public.

Afterward, I would return to my home, uphill and six blocks inland from McGinty's, open a Sam Adams, and sit in the living room staring at the harbor and the Atlantic Ocean beyond, remembering those carefree days before the Navy took Pete away to search for Nazi U-boats, when we spent days in his skiff, skinny-dipping in a secluded cove we discovered, and cooking fresh-caught fish over open fires on the beach. After the war, Pete did what every red-blooded American boy did back then: married and produced a new generation of Americans. His marriage was over long before he lost his leg, but he and his wife kept up appearances for years, she turning a blind eye to my relationship with Pete.

When his youngest daughter graduated high school, Pete left his wife and took a room on the second floor of McGinty's, where I had been working—first as a busboy and later as a bartender—ever since my 4F status prevented me from joining Pete on the front lines.

I often cadged two beers from the cooler and carried them upstairs to Pete's room. Some nights we would just sit and drink and talk and stare out at the harbor. Other nights we were more physical, and we made love until the wee hours of the morning when I had to slip out and return to my own home before the town awoke.

Late one fall afternoon, a few months after Pete had moved out, I saw a thirty-five-foot Beneteau First 35 motoring into the harbor, its sail down and a burly, dark-haired man at the wheel. I was headed in to work and I paused on the cobblestone street outside McGinty's to watch the sailboat dock and its lone occupant disembark. Somehow, I knew I would see him again later that day.

Had Pete still been around, he would have known everything there was to know about the stranger, and he would have shared that information with me before the man walked into McGinty's late that night and straddled the stool at the end of the bar under the Sam Adams sign, the same stool Pete had preferred during his days of beer drinking and tale spinning.

The stranger's black hair hung in ringlets to his broad shoulders and his beard brushed his thick chest whenever he moved his head. His skin, what was visible of it through the tattoo sleeves and the mask of hair, had been tanned the color of aged leather. He ordered dark rum and the tumbler in which I served it disappeared when he wrapped one meaty fist around the glass. Business was slow, with only locals occupying the place until the stranger's arrival, so I tried to engage him in conversation between orders. When I asked his name, he said, "People call me the captain."

I said, "I've not seen you here before."

"I don't usually sail this far north."

"So, where you from?"

"It's not where I'm from that's important," the captain said, "it's where I'm going."

I bit. "So, where are you going?"

He smiled through his beard. "We're all going the same place, John," he said, "eventually."

I replaced his empty tumbler with a fresh one and moved down the bar to wait on two brothers who were busy trying to drink each other under the table. Not until sometime later did I realize I hadn't told the captain my name and, unlike bartenders at hotels and chain restaurants, wasn't required to wear any form of name badge. I puzzled on that while I poured beer, freshened bar snacks, and swapped gossip with the sea-salted fishermen who found McGinty's a dark, wood-paneled purgatory between the hell of their homes and the heaven of the open sea.

When I finally returned to his end of the bar, the captain had finished his second tumbler of rum and was ready for a third. As I slid it across the worn wood of the bar, I asked, "Do we know each other from somewhere?"

"We've never met," he said, "but I know you."

Before I could follow up, one of the drunken brothers slapped the other end of the bar, startling me and causing me to turn.

"What're you mumbling about down there, old man?" he said. "Get us another round."

I moved down the bar. "You've had enough already," I suggested.

"Not if my brother's still standing," he insisted. "He doesn't have his beer legs yet."

After I glanced at my watch, I relented and opened two more bottles of Sam Adams. The brothers wouldn't have much longer to drink, and I knew if they didn't fall in the harbor as they wobbled down the dock, they could sleep it off on their boat.

The captain sat at the bar the rest of the night, nursing his rum and watching me work. No one approached him and no one spoke to him but me. He still occupied Pete's stool at last call and was still there at closing time a few minutes later after all the other patrons had been shooed out. I cashed out, switched off all but the night-lights, poured the last of the captain's rum in a clear plastic to-go cup, and escorted him to the exit.

When I opened the door to the street, I found Pete reaching for the knob. He wore cheap cotton pajamas with the nursing home logo printed over the left breast and he appeared clear-eyed and freshly shaven for the first time in more than a year. He stood in the open doorway, grabbed my head between his hands, and held it while he planted his lips on mine, right there in front of the captain. When he finally pulled his face back, Pete said, "I've missed you."

"I've missed you, too," I told him.

The captain said, "I'll wait."

Then he stepped past us and sat on the curb, his plastic cup of dark rum still gripped in one meaty fist.

After Pete entered the bar, I locked the door behind him. He took my hand and led me up the steps to the room that had been his. Once inside, he pushed me back against the door and kissed me again. His kiss was deep, penetrating, breath-stealing, and it filled me with the same desire and quivering anticipation that our assignations after skinny-dipping in the cove had all those years earlier, when our bodies had been young and hard, and we were still searching for ourselves.

He unbuttoned my shirt, pulled it free of my chinos, and pushed it off my shoulders. My undershirt followed, then my shoes, socks, chinos, and BVDs. His pajamas joined my clothing on the floor and, as our clothes fell away, so did our wrinkles and the ravages of aging. Perhaps it was just memories of better times clouding my vision, but I saw the young man I had fallen in love with rising naked from the water in our secluded cove, stepping off the Greyhound bus fresh from the war in his Navy dress whites, disembarking from one of the American seiners in his plaid wool shirt and jeans after a long day at sea.

His broad shoulders and thick chest tapered down to a flat stomach and narrow waist held aloft by powerful legs, and the mast that was his cock rose from the wild tangle of dark hair at his crotch without need of chemical assistance or manual manipulation, just as it had when we were young and still navigating the uncharted waters between lust and love.

As I dropped to my knees before Pete, I wrapped one hand around the thick shaft of his cock, surprised and delighted at how firm it felt in my fist. Several times I slid my fist up and down Pete's tumescent cock before I leaned forward and wrapped my lips around the spongy soft head. A bead of pre-come oozed out of the tip and I licked it away.

I slid my lips down Pete's mast, taking ever more of his cock into my mouth until I had to move my hand out of the way so that I could take it all in. Then I drew back until my teeth caught on his glans. I did it again and again and each time I took his entire length into my mouth, the dark tangle of Pete's pubic hair tickled my nose and his heavy balls bounced against my chin like a pair of boat fenders.

I wrapped my arms around his powerful thighs, caught his ass cheeks in my hands, and felt them tighten and relax as he began moving his hips forward and back, meeting my oral caresses with increasing vigor. When his ball sac began to tighten and he wrapped his thick fingers in my hair, I knew he wouldn't last much longer.

And he didn't. With one final thrust, he came, sending wave after wave of salty sperm splashing against the back of my throat. I swallowed and swallowed again, and when Pete's cock finally stopped spasming in my mouth, I pulled away and looked up at him.

He took my hand and helped me to my feet. Then he turned me around, and he stood behind me as we faced the window and looked across the harbor. Two dozen American seiners were lined up at the dock awaiting the crews that would take them to sea early the next morning, and I could see the captain's sailboat moored at the far end of the dock.

Pete leaned over my shoulder and whispered into my ear the same things he'd told me when we were younger, about how we'd been made for each other, how our love would allow us to overcome all obstacles, how we were as good as married even if no one else knew. "Look out there," he whispered as he pointed to the Atlantic Ocean beyond the entrance to the harbor. "What do you see?"

"Endless opportunity," I whispered in return, a call and response from our youth when our entire lives were ahead of us and not behind us.

He kissed my shoulder and the base of my neck. One arm wrapped around me and his strong fingers trailed down my chest, down my abdomen, to my erect cock. He wrapped his hand around it, nearly engulfing it in his big fist. As he continued kissing my neck and shoulder, he stroked my cock and I leaned back against him, comfortable in his arms. I had never had Pete's stamina and I came quickly, sending a thin stream of come shooting toward but not quite reaching the window.

By then Pete's mast had risen again and I could feel his cock snuggling between my ass cheeks. He stepped away and returned a moment later with a partial tube of lube, last used several months before he was taken to the nursing home. He uncapped it, coated his middle two fingers, and then slipped them down the length of my ass crack to my porthole of pleasure.

I bent forward and he massaged my sphincter until he could slip one finger into me. He continued his digital manipulation until he could also slip in his second finger. Then he withdrew them both, pressed his cock head against my lube-slickened hole, and pushed forward.

When he was deep inside me, just as he had been so many times in the past, every memory of our lovemaking flooded through my mind, from the first time as young men after skinny-dipping in the cove to the last time in Pete's room as old men barely able to coerce our cocks to attention. But what I remembered most were the good times, the best times, the times when we were young and could experience orgasm after orgasm as if they would have no end.

As I relived those memories, Pete stood behind me, holding my hips as if at the helm of a personal pleasure craft, and he steered us toward paradise, drawing back and pushing forward, moving slowly as if we had calm seas ahead of us forever.

But we didn't. He began moving faster, harder, driving into me, pounding into me, the rough seas of sex lashing against us, my own cock swelling again so that I had to take it in my hand, matching my rhythm to his as I jerked my mast, and I came, and Pete came, and he released inside me, and he held me until his cock stopped spasming and he could finally pull away.

We collapsed on his old bed and looked at each other, seeing what had been and not what was, and we held each other, feeling what had been and not what was, and we talked about what had been and not what was. For those few hours that one night we were young again, and we were whole again, but when it was over, we were old men again.

"I have to go now," Pete finally said. "The sea is calling."

He climbed from the bed and opened the closet, where some of his clothes remained because I could never find it within myself to discard them. He dressed carefully.

"Take me with you," I asked from the bed as he reached for the door.

Pete turned and said, "This trip's not for you."

He left me alone in his old room over the bar and clumped down the stairs.

I pushed myself off the bed and stepped to the window, where I watched the captain rise from the curb and take Pete's arm. Together they crossed the street and headed down the dock. The sound of Pete's wooden leg clicking against the cobblestones echoed through the still night air, replaced by the sound of his leg thumping against the weathered wood of the dock.

The captain helped Pete into his boat. Then he cast off and the Beneteau First 35 motored away from the dock. Once clear of the harbor, the mainsail rose, and I watched Pete and the captain sail into the rising sun.

I returned home before the town awoke and the dock filled with fishermen preparing for the day, and I didn't need to answer the ringing phone that greeted me when I pushed the door open to know that one of Pete's daughters was calling to tell me that Pete's ship had finally come for him.

Publishing Acknowledgments

"Learning Curve," *Daddy Knows Best,* Bruno Gmünder, 2013

"All-American Male," *Blowing Off Class*, Bruno Gmünder, 2014

"Discovering the Underground," *Big Man on Campus*, Cleis Press, 2013

"Come to Jesus," *Black Fire*, Bold Strokes Books, 2011

"Celebrity Crush," Original to this volume

"Boys of Summer," *Bad Boys*, Xcite, 2012

"Summer Folk," *Beach Bums*, Cleis Press, 2013

"Creosote Flats and the Big Spread," *The Handsome Prince*, Cleis Press, 2011

"What Springs Up," *Brief Encounters*, Cleis Press, 2011

"Relationships," *Steam Bath*, Cleis Press, 2013

"The XXXmas Gift," *Brief Encounters*, Cleis Press, 2011

"Friends and Lovers," *Lover Boys Forever*, StarBooks Press, 2013

"Riding Out the Storm," *Men*, February 2009

"Soaring," *Active Duty*, Cleis Press, 2014

"Flyboy," *Best Gay Romance 2015*, Cleis Press, 2015

"Memories," *Boys in Bed*, Xcite, 2013

"Blue Heart," *Take This Man*, Cleis Press, 2015

"Maryjane: Then and Now," *Drill Me Sergeant*, StarBooks Press, 2012

"Let Us Go Down to the Sea," *Sexy Sailors*, Cleis Press, 2012